heartbeats #1

Moving As One

Elizabeth M. Rees

Aladdin Paperbacks

To Jeni Breen and Linda Kessel
who continue to teach me
the joy of ballroom dancing

and

To Ian Folker
who generously gave of his time,
sharing his knowledge and enthusiasm for the art

First Aladdin Paperbacks edition August 1998

Copyright © 1998 by Elizabeth Marraffino

Aladdin Paperbacks
An imprint of Simon & Schuster Children's Publishing Division
1230 Avenue of the Americas
New York, NY 10020

Designed by Steve Scott
The text for this book was set in New Times Roman.
Printed and bound in the United States of America
10 9 8 7 6 5 4 3 2 1

Library of Congress Cataloging-in-Publication Data
Rees, Elizabeth M.
Moving as one / by Elizabeth M. Rees.
p.   cm. — (Heart beats ; #1)
Summary: Seventeen-year-old Carlos and sixteen-year-old Sophy find
each other arrogant and snobbish at first, but when his ballroom danc-
ing school merges with her ballet school, they must deal with a grow-
ing mutual attraction.
ISBN 0-689-81948-X (pbk.)
[1. Ballet dancing—Fiction. 2. Ballroom dancing—Fiction.] I. Title.
II. Series: Rees, Elizabeth M. Heart beats ; #1.
PZ7.R25476Mo   1998
[Fic]—dc21   98-17136
CIP   AC

Chapter One

The day disaster struck for the second time in Sophy Bartlett's life, the riverfront town of High Falls, Pennsylvania, was under a flood watch. Rain had fallen steadily for three days. Although the Ballet Academy, which was located in a converted warehouse down by the river, canceled its regular classes, Sophy couldn't bear staying home and missing even a day of barre work. So she splashed across a parking lot that resembled a lake, and found the building open and the studios empty.

Even with the lights on, the spacious studio looked dreary in the rain, and the tall windows lining one wall were drafty. Sweat, rosin, and the odor of dusting powder hung in the air after last night's classes. The familiar smells were sweet to Sophy. Pulling a teal-blue sweatshirt over her black leotard, Sophy thought about how much she loved this place, and how lucky she was that one of the best classical ballet schools in the Northeast was in her hometown.

As she twined the satin ribbons of her pointe shoes snugly around her ankles, Sophy looked at the clock and sighed. She had promised her best friend, Daly Flanagan, a private coaching session. Sophy was a firm believer in keeping promises. Daly, however, was not a firm believer in being on time.

Still, Sophy didn't mind the wait. She sat on the floor and began her familiar warm-up routine. With the soles of her feet together, she pressed her knees toward the floor to loosen her hips, then she extended her legs out, first working her ankles in circles to warm up her feet, then she stretched her hamstrings and back.

The warm-up completed, Sophy scrambled to her feet, adjusted the narrow band of elastic pinned around her slender waist, and headed for the barre. She pressed a button on the tape deck to rewind the practice cassette. While she waited for the music to start, Sophy stepped up on pointe and stretched one leg into a long arabesque. She checked her reflection in the mirror, her smoky-gray eyes serious. Carefully she corrected her line, lifting the toe of her raised leg a bit higher, pulling her weight up off her slim hips. Slowly, she took her hand off the barre and held the balance perfectly on one foot, counting out the beats in her head: one, two, three, four.

All right! Smiling, Sophy dropped out of position and curtsied to herself. "Bartlett, now *that* really was worthy of Fonteyn!" she told her reflection. Margot Fonteyn, the legendary British ballerina, was Sophy's idol. Sophy had watched her performances endlessly on video. People even told her she resembled Fonteyn, with her darkish hair, fair skin, and perfect dancer's build: naturally slim, five foot four, and classical proportions. To be a great ballerina like Fonteyn—that was Sophy's dream.

Well, she thought with an embarrassed laugh. She sure had a long way to go for that. With hard work and a very big break, she'd be lucky to make it into the corps of a national ballet company in the next couple of years. Still—*an arabesque Fonteyn would be proud of.* That's what Alexander Davidoff, head of the nationally renowned Empire State Ballet, had told Sophy just a week ago during the last class of Summerdance, the advanced summer workshop she had attended back in New York.

Sophy would treasure that compliment for the rest of her life. It was the second time he had complimented her. Once, he had told her her bourrées were soft as silk.

Of course, there was that *other* comment. Every time Sophy thought of it her stomach went a bit queasy. What had Davidoff been talking about? *Sophy, you have the heart of a dancer,* he'd said, *but you still need to learn to dance from your heart.*

The tape deck clicked, then whirred. Finally the soulful strains of a slow Chopin waltz rose from the speakers. The music made her worries about Davidoff fade. Tugging down the back of her leotard, Sophy sank gracefully into a demi-plié. Before she completed the move, the studio door squeaked open.

Sophy looked over her shoulder. "Daly!" she

called out. "Late is one thing, but twenty minutes—" she scolded cheerfully, turning off the cassette. Daly flipped back the hood of her bright blue poncho. A cloud of pale blond hair tumbled to her shoulders. Sophy stopped smiling. Daly's blue eyes were red and swollen. "Daly, what's wrong?" Sophy cried, hurrying across the room.

Daly stared woefully at Sophy, then burst into tears. "Something—something terrible," she sobbed. "Oh, Sophy what are we going to do?" Suddenly she brushed away her tears and put her fingers to her lips. Then she went to the studio door and poked her head outside. "No one's here?" she whispered. "You're alone?"

"Someone's home upstairs. I heard footsteps," Sophy said, fishing tissues out of a box on the piano and handing them to Daly. The directors of the Ballet Academy, Peter and Jan MacGregor, had an apartment on the top floor of the loft building.

Daly blotted her eyes, careful not to smear her mascara, then blew her nose. "Sophy," she said in a hoarse whisper, "you'd better sit down." Daly took off her poncho and dropped down on the floor, just under the barre, with her back against the wall.

Sophy sat cross-legged beside her and butted her shoulder against Daly's. "Hey, girlfriend, you're scaring me," she said. Daly sure looked pretty tragic. "Something happen at home?" Sophy asked, afraid to hear the answer. As far as she knew, the Flanagans were a pretty tight family, but Sophy never trusted what families looked like from the outside. Before her own parents split up, everyone thought the Bartletts were from sitcom central.

"No, it's nothing like that," Daly said. "It's the school."

"Lincoln High?" Sophy asked, puzzled. School wouldn't open until next week, after Labor Day. "Are the teachers on strike? Something like that?"

"No. It's the *Academy*"—Daly's eyes brimmed with tears—"it's closing!"

"Come off it, Daly," Sophy scoffed. "That's, like, a really bad joke."

"I'm *not* joking."

Sophy stared at her friend. Daly looked positively ashen. It was as if someone had died. "You're not . . . I—I don't understand." Sophy felt as if the floor beneath her had turned to quicksand. "My mom filled out the forms for the new school year just yesterday—the stuff for scholarships and all that. I'm signed up for pointe class and adagio and"— Sophy's mouth went dry—"what happened?" And then she added half to herself—"How could Mom not tell me?"

"She doesn't know—not yet," Daly explained. "She'll hear tomorrow—or tonight. All the parents will."

"How did you find out?"

"Besides the fact I'm High Falls's walking teenage grapevine?" Daly laughed a little sharply. "Laverne called me just now."

"Laverne Grey?" Sophy's racing heart began to

slow. Laverne was a terrific dancer and a good friend, but not the most reliable person at the Academy. She was known for playing some pretty wild practical jokes.

"It's not what you're thinking," Daly said quickly. "Laverne's not making this one up. Her father might be out of a job as of next week. She's completely freaked. She's been filling in at the reception desk over the summer to earn some money. Today she accidently overheard a phone conversation. Apparently the Academy is in serious financial trouble—"

"That's old news," Sophy said, sure that Daly or Laverne must be exaggerating. "I know the High Falls Ballet Company lost its grant in July. But that's supposed to be temporary. That big office-supply chain was talking about backing them in time for this season's *Nutcracker*."

Sophy remembered the whole incident very well. Her mother was on the board of the High Falls Ballet Company. Anne Bartlett herself had told Sophy there was nothing to worry about.

"So," Sophy asked Daly, "what's the Company grant have to do with the school?"

"Nothing," Daly said miserably. "Except that the school's grant didn't come through, either, and today the bank turned down the MacGregors's loan application. They have to close down—maybe even sell the building. I don't know."

"This can't be happening." Sophy squeezed her

eyes shut tight and held her breath a minute. Then she opened her eyes. Rain was still pounding the tall windows, and wind whooshed down the alleys near the waterfront. She was still in the same corner studio of the Ballet Academy. Daly was sitting next to her. This was real. Not a dream.

Daly swallowed hard. "Worst part is they won't even open next week for the new term."

"No classes. Not even next week?" Sophy stared bleakly at Daly. "What are we going to do? Where will we take classes? There isn't a school within twenty miles that's half as good."

"I know," Daly sighed, and propped her head against her friend's shoulder. "Until today I thought I wouldn't care so much if something came along to get in the way of becoming a dancer. I sort of prayed somehow the decision would be taken out of my hands."

Sophy's eyebrows rose in shock.

"Don't!" Daly wailed. "Don't look at me that way. I'm not you, Sophy. No one in this school is. You're the best dancer who's come along in years. Everyone says that—"

"Stop it!" Sophy protested. "That's not true. I just work harder than most people, including you." Daly's only problems were keeping her weight down and a lazy streak. Most of the advanced scholarship students were already nearly good enough to try out for professional companies.

Not that it mattered now. Sophy's voice was flat

with despair. "Without the school, I might as well give up. Davidoff told me I had to work very, very hard this year. Learn everything I could here. Then maybe next spring I could start trying out for the companies. But now—"

Daly flung her arms around Sophy. "Somehow, some way, something will work out—at least for you. You're born to dance, Soph."

Tears gathered behind Sophy's eyes, but she was too numb to cry. Only a few minutes ago she'd been dreaming of being the next Fonteyn. She had been wondering how to put more heart in her dancing.

And now? Sophy felt as if someone had just ripped the heart right out of her.

♡ ♡ ♡

In Carlos Vargas's arms I can be anything. Light as a whisper. Secret as smoke. Roxanna Ivanov softly placed her fingers on Carlos's shoulder as they danced the tango. His hand was firm on her back, their bodies pressed into each other as he led her across the smooth floor of the small ballroom dancing studio. Nadia Ivanov, Roxy's mother and coach, had been inspired when she teamed them up last June. In less than three months they had almost perfected their competitive dance routines. Already they moved together as one.

Too bad Carlos hadn't figured out they should be an item off the dance floor as well as on. His hold around Roxanna tightened slightly as he maneuvered her through a complex series of steps. Eyes half closed, Roxanna imagined him holding her just this way somewhere private, romantic, moonlit— like the gazebo on the banks of Riverfront Park. She inhaled the musky scent of his aftershave and lost her concentration.

Roxanna stumbled slightly and twisted her ankle. "Rats!" she grumbled, limping off a little ways.

"Earth to Ivanov!" Carlos said, sounding exasperated. "What's with you tonight?" He flicked off the CD player.

"I just slipped," she retorted a bit defensively, then exaggerated her limp.

"Hey, you hurt your ankle!" he said, quickly taking her arm. "Is it bad?" He supported her while she massaged her ankle with her other hand.

She was just fine, but hesitated before she answered. "I—I don't think so." Leaning against his chest, she experimented working her foot around in little circles. Slowly she smiled, glancing at Carlos through her long dark lashes. "I'm okay—really— I'm tougher than I look!" She tightened her fist and made a muscle in her arm. "You know that."

Carlos arched one eyebrow. "Should I?" He gently felt her muscle. A delicious shiver cascaded from the top of her head to the bottom of her spine. "Impressive!" he said with a small smile.

So Mr. Machismo does *know how to flirt!* She stepped away from him and tried a couple of swerving steps. "Let's try it again—but this time don't trick me," she purred.

Carlos looked up from reselecting the CD track and laughed. "Come off it, Roxy. I wasn't tricking you," he said, reaching for her hand and walking to the far end of the dance floor. "I was *leading* you."

"Through something we've never done before. Don't pull that in competition." She pretended to look angry. But she squeezed his hand reassuringly, and as the music began they resumed the dance.

Expertly Roxanna followed his lead, thinking wherever this guy might lead her, she would gladly follow. Though she'd prefer it if he'd lead her clear outside the cramped studios of Rainbow Dance and waltz her right across the whole dreary state of Pennsylvania, straight onto the floor of the grand ballroom of the Ohio Star Ball. Someday they'd tango across TV screens as reigning National Ballroom Champions.

Roxanna's number one dream was of fame, glory, and tons of money. She was determined to be a star on the ballroom circuit, maybe even win gold at the Olympics. She was not going to be like her parents, working themselves to the bone to run this rinky-dink dance school. Until the recent ballroom fad kicked in, the family had been on the verge of bankruptcy.

Roxanna's number two dream was currently in her arms. Sultry, talented Carlos.

Crush at first sight, Roxanna thought, but now the crush of a ten-year-old had turned into something else. She was sixteen going on seventeen, and her feelings for Carlos had blossomed into more than just infatuation. She was in love with him. She was absolutely sure of that. Besides, crushes were temporary, and Roxanna intended her partnership with Carlos on and off the dance floor to be *permanent*. To that end, she refocused herself on their dancing. As he guided her through a new pattern of steps, her body was in perfect sync with his. Lightly, she embellished the intricate footwork.

"That was really hot!" he said as they finished. Still holding her hand, he turned her so they both faced the mirror that ran the length of one studio wall. "Run those steps by me one more time."

"Sure," she answered his reflection in the mirror. As she demonstrated the movement, she thought they made a great-looking couple. An *almost* matched pair: both dark, both passionate. Roxanna had big hair: curly, deep brown, long, gorgeous. His black hair was cropped short, but curled slightly at the nape of his neck. His eyes were dark, sparkling, full of wonder and fun. Hers, set above high Slavic cheekbones, were almond shaped, deep brown, mysterious. She was trim and strong, but with a very curvy figure. He was thin, all edges, angles. His true beauty was in the way he held himself. Roxy's mother, their teacher, always said Carlos had the kind of posture that made him look more like a prince than the son of an auto mechanic.

Carlos checked the clock on the wall and frowned. "Time's almost up. The after-work crowd is about to mob the studio!" he joked. "Let's try to work in a couple more quick run-throughs."

"I'm game," Roxanna responded as another tango track began.

He wrapped his arm around her. Her palm was pressed against his, and their foreheads were barely inches apart as the slow, moody music crescendoed. Roxanna suddenly found herself slightly breathless. She'd been nuts about Carlos since he was ten. That's how old he'd been when he had turned up shabby and scrawny in a patched denim jacket, holding his equally scrawny sister by the hand. He'd begged for chores at Rainbow Dance in exchange for lessons. His sheer guts had impressed Roxanna's mother enough to give him *and* his sister full scholarships. In less than a year, Carlos Vargas was dancing in kids' competitions with his sister. Now, at seventeen, he had proven to be the most talented competitive dancer in the junior division of the local amateur ballroom circuit. And that was back when he was still dancing with his sister! Roxanna smiled, thinking to herself: *Those judges ain't seen nothing yet— just wait until they see Ivanov and Vargas!*

What a team they made!

Abruptly, the tape ended, leaving only the rhythm of rain beating the windows and the sound of the crowd in the hallways arriving for evening classes. For a measure or two they continued the pattern of *ochos*—steps that traced a complicated series of figure eights—then stopped. For barely an instant, they were still locked in a tango hold.

Roxanna could feel Carlos's heart pounding against her chest, the heat of his breath against her face. As she lifted her eyes toward him she saw little beads of sweat on his forehead, his hair clinging in damp curls to the back of his neck. His mouth hovered inches from hers.

Bewitched, Roxanna reached up and brushed her lips against his. For a moment his arm tightened around her shoulders, then he kissed her back. The slow, surprise kiss sent blood rushing to Roxanna's head. She felt almost faint and, when he stepped back suddenly, she had to grab his arms to keep from losing her balance.

Carlos looked embarrassed and a little flustered. "Hey, Roxy," he said, not quite meeting her eyes. "*That's* not a good idea. Not for partners, and not for us. Remember what your mom says: *In tango the passion is all pretend.*"

"Carlos, I wasn't pretending," Roxanna whispered hoarsely.

He slipped out of her reach and averted his eyes. When he looked up, his cheeks were flushed and he seemed confused. "I know. It felt nice. Listen, any guy would enjoy kissing you—you're great. But even if it weren't better for dance partners not to get involved with each other, I'm not interested, Roxanna. Not that way. You're a good *friend*—okay?"

Roxanna's face began to burn. "Sure. Whatever you say."

Carlos turned away to rewind the tape. "That wasn't a bad run-through," he said. "Want to take it from the top one more time before your mother comes back?"

Roxanna nodded. She walked over to the window, furious with herself for acting the fool and not at all convinced Carlos knew his own feelings. The damp breeze blew through the screen, cooling her face. How could Carlos lie to himself? He *had* kissed her back, big-time, at least for a second. If that was pretend, then she had two heads, four legs, and hailed from Mars.

The insistent tango music started again. She turned. Carlos held out his hand, smiling as if nothing had just happened between them. Roxanna returned a cool smile. If it was pretend he wanted, she'd pretend. Pretend she wasn't head over heels in love with him.

"Let's work out that pattern again," he said.

She took a deep breath and stepped into his arms, wondering how this guy could act as if tango dancing were all business.

"Wrong, wrong, *wrong!*" a heavily accented voice shouted from across the studio.

Roxanna cringed at the sound. "Now what!" she groaned, stopping in her steps and turning to face her mother. They had the same mysterious almond-shaped eyes, the same high Slavic cheekbones, but Nadia Ivanov was fair, and thin as a stick, with a boyish figure and a straight, narrow mouth.

"I leave the room for five minutes and you make the steps all wrong. You dance like lead in your legs, Miss Ivanov. What is all this distance between you?" Nadia Ivanov crossed the room and stepped between Roxanna and Carlos. "It is like this." She rested her left hand lightly on Carlos's shoulders, her fingers brushing the nape of his neck. She stepped closer until their torsos were lightly touching. Her right hand rested in his left; her forehead grazed his.

"See," she said, then stepped aside.

Roxanna swallowed hard, then imitated her mother's position. "Like this?" she murmured, half into Carlos's face. As she rested her hand on his shoulder, his muscles tensed ever so slightly. Roxanna smiled to herself. *If he's fighting me, there must something to fight,* she figured. He was attracted. He could battle his feelings all he wanted. Eventually, Roxanna was sure he'd give in. They danced together so perfectly, it was obvious they were meant to be together.

Her mother adjusted their position and turned the tape back on. The passionate tempo set Roxanna's pulse racing, and she moved as if the music were playing inside her back, her arms, her legs, her heart. But Carlos felt like wood.

They danced a few measures when her mother stopped the music. "No. Something is wrong. You have danced already this piece a hundred times, and a hundred times better than this. Where is Inez?" Nadia cried.

Roxanna barely smothered a groan. Not Inez. Not now. She folded her arms across her chest. "Off in studio two doing a barre," she answered scornfully.

"Barre work?" Nadia repeated.

Carlos glanced up sharply.

"Or whatever," Roxanna mumbled, avoiding her mother's eyes.

The door to the studio opened, and a fragile-looking Latina girl walked in. "Sorry, Mrs. Ivanov, were you looking for me?" she asked.

"Yes. When you wait for your partner—" Nadia broke off to check her watch. Then nodded. "Brad's not out of school yet," she remarked. "But as I say, when you wait for partner, you do not waste time. You should dance here to the music, without partner. Understand?"

"Yes, Mrs. Ivanov, but I was—"

"Whatever, dance now with Carlos. You," she said, turning to Roxanna, "watch carefully. Inez has the movements perfectly."

"Yeah, right!" Roxanna grunted, and leaned back to watch them. *Let them trip,* she prayed.

Of course they didn't. The music barely started, and they were moving in a smooth, sinuous pattern across the floor. Carlos led his sister seamlessly through a series of complex steps, footwork, and turns. Roxanna's expert eye couldn't detect the slightest flaw in their dancing. Though you'd have to be blind not to see their tango was too platonic. It lacked fire. That's why Inez and Carlos weren't teamed up for competitions anymore. They had style, technique, but no magic.

With me, you're all magic, Roxanne silently told Carlos as the music stopped.

"You see the difference?" her mother was saying.

"Mrs. Ivanov, the phone," someone called from the hall.

The dance teacher was barely out of the room when Roxanna treated Inez to a sugary smile. "Nicely done, Inez. Very sweet."

"Sweet?" Carlos echoed, sounding annoyed. "Tango isn't *sweet.*"

"Exactly," Roxanna murmured. "But then, Inez doesn't really want to dance tango. All she wants is to be some airhead ballerina."

"Ballerinas aren't airheads," Inez spoke up. "They—"

Ignoring Inez, Roxanna turned to Carlos. "Hasn't your sister told you her big secret?"

"What secret?" Carlos asked, staring at Inez.

"I don't know," Inez stammered, her cheeks growing pink.

"Oh—so it's not a secret," Roxanna said. "I guess it doesn't matter who knows about your private ballet lessons with my dad!"

Inez gasped. "How'd you find out about that?"

"I have my ways of finding out about things around here. And I've seen plenty, Inez. Not that you're bad, but everyone knows three dumb classes a week aren't enough to make a ballerina out of a born genius, let alone you. I mean, what exactly is the point?"

"Stop it, Roxanna. Just stop it!" Inez shouted. Tears streamed from her eyes, and she rushed from the room.

"Inez?" Carlos called, then ran after her.

"Carlos, come back here. We have to practice!" Roxanna shouted as the door slammed behind Carlos.

Roxanna stood alone, fuming, in the middle of the studio. Suddenly the tape deck clicked and shifted into replay. Loud strains of tango blared from the speakers. Roxanna glared at the machine and stamped her foot.

"Stop it!" she shouted, yanking off one high heel and hurling it at the tape player. The shoe thwacked the wall, but the passionate music continued, as if mocking her.

Chapter Two

"Inez?" Carlos pushed his way through the crowded hallway. He was furious with Roxanna and annoyed at himself. He should have seen it coming. Roxanna had been throwing herself at him for weeks, but he'd pretended it was only the make-believe passion of the dance. And, he had to admit to himself, he had sort of enjoyed the attention.

Roxanna was drop-dead gorgeous. A perfect ten in most guys' books. If they weren't partners, he might have let that kiss go a little further.

"Inez?" Carlos called again, but his voice was swallowed in the din. African drumming thumped out of one studio. A slow waltz curled out of another. Hot thirties jazz tunes shook the walls of the studio where a swing class was revving up.

Well, what happened had happened, Carlos told himself. He could be professional enough to deal with it. He'd been around the ballroom scene long enough to see partners get involved, then break up and have all sorts of problems dancing with each other after that. Roxanna was ambitious enough for their partnership to survive; she'd learn to live with being just friends.

He *did* want to dance with her. They were already

dynamite on the dance floor. With a few more months of practice, they'd be ready to wow the judges and crowds. And Carlos loved the competitions—the challenge, the excitement, the suspense. He was determined to become great. Famous, even.

Still, Roxanna had no right to take out her frustrations on his sister.

"Vargas," Eric Anders called out from behind the sign-in desk. "Don't forget you're covering the eight P.M. salsa class for Meredith. She got stranded by the storm."

"Right!" What rotten timing! He'd actually forgotten about subbing tonight. Now he couldn't lure Inez out of the studio down to The Beggar's Bean for coffee and talk.

The eight o'clock crowd was already mobbed at the sign-in desk for the next hour of classes. In spite of the terrible weather the school was open for business, and every studio in Rainbow Dance was bursting with students, as usual. Carlos had to fairly elbow his way into the short back hall.

"Inez?" he called for the umpteenth time, then opened the closet sandwiched between the small office and the reception area of the school. "You in here?"

Above the sound of salsa music filtering through the wall of the adjacent studio, he detected muffled sobs. He shouldered his way between two racks of sequined and feathered ballroom dresses. A floor-to-ceiling shelf was built into the back wall. It was filled with assorted dancing shoes, mainly women's heels, in silver, gold, or satiny colors. Next to the shelf was a large wicker trunk. Inez sat on the floor beside it. Her head was pillowed in her arms, her shoulders racked with sobs.

"*¿Hermanita, qué pasa?* Little sister, what's going on?" Carlos asked softly, hunkering down on the floor next to her. He touched her shoulder, then smoothed her dark, curly hair.

"I don't want to talk about it," Inez whispered between sobs. "She's so mean."

"Roxanna?" Carlos inhaled deeply. "Don't let her get to you." He weighed his next words carefully. "She was just frustrated with me. We had some problems rehearsing today. She's jealous, that's all. That you and I still dance better together."

"Jealous? Of me?" Inez looked up, her dark eyes blazing. "Come off it, Carlos. She's a better ballroom dancer than I am, and you guys are still just new to each other." Inez rubbed her thin arm across her face and sniffed back tears. "With you she's got her career as a National Ballroom Champion made. Why do you think her mother paired her up with you? A person would have to be blind not to see you were made for each other."

Made to dance *with each other,* Carlos silently corrected her as Inez went on. "Look, I'm okay now. She was just—oh, so nasty. I don't want to talk about it."

"I do," Carlos said quietly, sitting on the trunk

beside her. "What was this about ballet lessons with her dad?"

Inez gulped audibly. "It's true," she said after a long pause.

"When are these lessons?" Carlos felt annoyed and confused. "When do you have time?"

"I—I come here early before school. And then on Saturdays. But she's right, you know. Even studying with Mikhail Ivanov, I can't get good enough dancing three hours a week. I should quit now, before I make more of a fool of myself."

The bitterness in his sister's voice left Carlos at a loss for words. "You want to dance ballet that much? How come I didn't know this?" He'd always thought Inez wanted to be a ballroom dancer just like him.

Inez looked up at Carlos, her eyes swimming with tears. "I didn't want to disappoint you."

"Disappoint *me?*" He took his sister's face between his hands and stared earnestly into her big dark eyes. "All I want is for you to be happy. I never dreamed you didn't love ballroom dancing. You dance so well, and—"

"Oh, I do love it, but not as much as ballet." Inez gave a little shiver. When she looked up at him again her eyes were sparkling. "Remember when we were little—I think I was only six—and I won those dance classes at the Ballet Academy?"

"When the school was still at the mall?" How could he forget? It was just before the prestigious ballet school had relocated to the renovated ware-house down by the riverfront.

His mother had entered a contest sponsored by a supermarket and won three months of weekly ballet lessons for Inez. While his mother had worked Saturday mornings, he'd had to stay at the mall until Inez had finished her class. He had watched the classes avidly; at home he had practiced all the steps. Inez's classes had sparked his own passion for dance. Two years later he'd gotten up the courage to go to Rainbow Dance and bargain for free lessons for them both.

"Even after the ballet lessons ended, I kept prac-ticing those steps," Inez confessed. "One day, here, when I was about ten, I was doing pliés when no one was around. Mikhail saw me and told me I was doing them all wrong. That's when he began giving me exercises. At first I practiced only at home, but the past couple of years, he's been giving me lessons—like Roxanna said," Inez admitted rueful-ly. "Three times a week—I'm not bad, but she is right, you know. It's pretty dumb to dream I could become a ballerina."

"A ballerina." Carlos looked more carefully at his sister. She was graceful, with long legs, a long neck, and a delicate yet strong body. "What does Mikhail say?" he asked.

"Mikhail?" Inez smiled shyly. "He says, with training, I might have made a real dancer."

Mikhail Ivanov was a rising ballet star back

when Russia was still the Soviet Union, before he was hurt in a terrible accident. He'd given up his career. He didn't even teach dancing anymore. Besides helping administer the ballroom school with his wife, he drove a cab. Still, if Mikhail thought Inez had a chance—Carlos's mind began to race. Ballet lessons. Lots of them. Every day. Unless Inez had some kind of scholarship, that seemed impossible, but still. . . .

Carlos got to his feet. He reached for his sister's hand and pulled her up beside him. "If Mikhail Ivanov believes you're good enough to be a ballet dancer, you shouldn't give up," he said. "You'll find a way."

"How, Carlos?" Inez asked despairingly. "There's no money, and here I take all the ballroom classes for free. Nadia is grooming me for the Nationals. Besides, I'd rather dance ballroom than nothing at all."

"I know all that," Carlos said impatiently. "Just don't give up, okay?" He tugged on a strand of her hair and grinned at her. "Maybe there's a way to make this *loco* dream of yours come true."

Inez grinned back at him. "I think you're the one who's *loco.*"

"Maybe," Carlos admitted. "But you know, *hermanita,* I'm a dreamer. So you just keep dancing with Mikhail." He lowered his voice to a conspiratorial whisper. "I promise I won't tell anyone your secret."

But to himself he vowed, somehow, some way, his sister wouldn't have to keep her secret for long.

♡ ♡ ♡

That evening Sophy sat in her top-floor bedroom, trying to sew ribbons on her pointe shoes. This annual fall ritual had always signaled the end of the summer and the start of a new, exciting round of dance classes. But, now—

"Why bother?" Sophy asked aloud, and threw the pink satin shoe across the room. It skidded across the gray-and-black throw rug, under the bookshelf. One half-sewn ribbon trailed out onto the polished broad-planked floor.

"I hate this year. I hate my life. I hate everything!" Sophy complained loudly.

Furiously, she began shoving the two dozen pairs of new toe shoes back into a plastic bag. To think that just a week ago she'd been so proud of being such a smart shopper, going with one of the other Summerdance apprentices on a subway out to Queens in New York to buy shoes by the dozen, at a discount. Even her mother had been impressed at the savings. Now she had enough toe shoes to last her for most of the school year—shoes she might as well throw in the garbage!

How could life be so unfair? Sophy asked herself. What had she done to deserve such a bad break? It wasn't as if her dance career had always been smooth. She'd had her share of minor injuries. She'd lost some parts to other girls in the school, though not lately. In spite of her gifts, not every new combination came easy to her. But she had learned early on that hard work, determination, and a never-give-up attitude got her through most tough spots. Taking charge made her feel strong, and she loved it. Her fate, she decided ages ago, was in her own hands.

Or had been until today. Now her whole life was on the line because of some dumb money problems at the Academy. Stuff she not only couldn't control, but couldn't even begin to understand.

Seething, she reached over to retrieve her shoe from under the white-painted bookshelf. Relics of her childhood were propped between and in front of books on the bottom shelf: a ragged stuffed dog; her first tiny ballet slippers; a brightly painted clay dish she'd made in art camp. But mostly photos, scads of them. Sophy adored pictures and scrounged the riverfront flea markets for cheap, vintage frames.

Her shelf, desk, and walls were adorned with snapshots: of her and Daly. Her and her mom. Her grandparents on their fortieth wedding anniversary just last year. Sophy and her kid sister, Emma, taken back in May when Emma was all dressed up for her first boy-girl dance. And her favorite: the picture of Sophy with her dad. It was more than ten years old now, and the cheap color print was fading, but the photo was one of Sophy's most treasured possessions. In it her father towered over her, holding her tiny hand. She was a thin, waiflike six-year-old, with huge dark eyes. "Just how you'd imagine an orphan would look!" Daly used to tease her. Sophy's father had a mop of blond curly hair, blue eyes, a lighthearted smile, and no more resembled her than any other stranger. But he wasn't a stranger; he was the daddy whom she had adored more than anyone in the world.

Then one morning, a week or so after she had begun first grade, her mother told her he was gone. Why? Where? Sophy still had no idea. But she could still remember how she'd felt: as if her insides had been scooped away like the heart of a pumpkin.

Exactly the way she felt now. The Academy was closing, and Sophy had no idea what would become of her. She wished she could just up and run away somewhere—people ran off to join the circus. Maybe she could run off and join Empire State Ballet in New York. She gripped the framed photo of her father harder, and the tight knot of tears that had been building since that afternoon finally loosened. She clapped her hand over her mouth and let out a hurt cry, then flung herself facedown on her arms and sobbed like she hadn't in ten years.

"Sophy!" Emma called from downstairs. "You've got company."

Sitting up quickly, Sophy hid the photo behind some books and gulped back her tears. Not Daly. Not now. Sophy scrambled to her feet and rubbed the sleeve of her old flannel shirt across her face.

Then Daly was banging at her bedroom door.

"It's open," Sophy called, wishing for once she had the nerve to tell Daly to go home. Just thinking that made Sophy hate herself. For some reason the news about the school had made her furious with Daly, with her mother, with Emma, with everyone.

Daly poked her head in the room, her round face sunny. At the sight of Sophy, the sparkle went out of her eyes. "Oh, Soph, it's not *that* bad."

"What's not bad about it?" Sophy retorted as she went back to putting away her shoes. "Or has High Falls Savings and Loan had a change of heart?"

"Look," Daly said, stooping down to help Sophy. "First of all, this just happened. I think all the parents are really freaked—mine are, at any rate—about this. Give people a chance to work things out. We can't give up yet, not so fast." Daly sat back on her heels, regarding her friend's swollen eyes. "It's not like you to cave in like this."

"Get real, Daly!" Sophy half shouted, then bit her lip. "Sorry. Didn't mean to snap. I'm just"—she fiddled with the little hole in the knee of her jeans—"I don't see what *we* can do about any of this. Our families can't even afford to pay for all our classes. So where's the money going to come from to keep the Academy open? If the banks don't think the school has a chance—who will?" Sophy fought back the sob rising from her chest. "What's there to be hopeful about?"

"Your mother," Daly replied instantly. "And lots of other parents, too. If the Academy really closes, the only ballet school within twenty miles will be that little storefront at the Riverview Mall."

"*Danceland?*" Sophy said scornfully. "*I* could teach there. The people who run that place never danced in a ballet company in their lives. I think one of the women who owns the place used to be a Rockette, or something like that."

"Rockettes are real dancers," Daly pointed out. "I wouldn't mind being one myself if my legs were long enough." She tossed a toe shoe at Sophy. "You're turning into even more of a ballet snob since you came back from New York."

Sophy made a face. "I know," she admitted with a small smile. "But, Daly, don't you understand? I just want to be the best, and to be one of the best you need the most serious dance education you can get. I need teachers who will push me to my limits. You can't blame me for wanting that."

"I know," Daly said in a sympathetic tone. "But I still think some dance is better than none at all."

Sophy was too tired to argue the point. Besides, sometimes she thought no one, not even her best friend, really understood her ambition. Sophy didn't want to be just a good dancer. She was determined to be a great ballerina. Glumly, she twirled the floppy ears of her fuzzy bunny rabbit slippers.

Daly packed up the last of the shoes and handed the bag to Sophy. "But as for Danceland," she said, flopping down on the window seat, "no one in this town is going to want to drag their eight-year-olds that far twice a week after school. My mom was talking to your mom earlier. They're trying to arrange a meeting of faculty, students, and parents next week." Daly paused, then added, "When *Professor* Bartlett gets involved, things start happening."

"True," Sophy said, feeling a glimmer of hope. In a no-win situation her mother wouldn't waste time trying to make things work. For better or worse, that simply wasn't Anne Bartlett's style. "So maybe with Mom onboard," Sophy finally admitted, "we shouldn't give up yet."

Daly pumped her arms in the air. "Yeah. The old Sophy is back!"

Chapter Three

Now this *is more like it!* Carlos thought as he parked the vintage black pickup in the parking lot of the High Falls Ballet Academy. The warehouse on the corner of Canal and Green was in dire need of paint, but the huge loft building was Carlos's dream come true. If he were rich, he'd write a check tonight and buy the place, as is.

As he jogged up the front steps of the school, his car keys jangling in his jeans pocket, he laughed out loud. "Rich" was barely a word he could afford in his vocabulary. He was seventeen, still in high school, without so much as a checking account to his name. Nevertheless Carlos was a strong believer in dreams. The Academy, with its tall windows, tawny in the golden sunset, promised to be huge inside with space for ten dance schools. Just looking at it now firmed up the vague ideas drifting in his mind. Carlos had passed the place a zillion times, but had scarcely bothered to look at it. Until this evening.

To think it was just a week since he'd overheard the gossip in school. The High Falls Ballet Academy was going bust. Raul Gomez's brother, a caretaker at the dance school, was worried about his job. Then Carlos saw an announcement about tonight's meeting—a meeting open to the *whole* High Falls community. For the life of him, Carlos had no idea what he would do or say at the meeting, but he had a strong gut feeling, a sixth sense he'd learned years ago never to ignore. A voice inside that said his luck, his life, was about to change.

Last time he'd felt that way, he'd been ten years old knocking on the door of Rainbow Dance, begging for lessons.

Inside the Academy, signs posted in the foyer pointed the way toward the auditorium. A short walk down the hall and he found himself standing in the doorway of a small theater with rows of seats and a stage. The curtain was open to reveal a table, a row of folding chairs, and a podium with a microphone. Half a dozen people were milling around the stage. Carlos quickly picked out the directors of the school, Jan and Peter MacGregor. He had seen them at Rainbow Dance now and then on showcase nights.

Although the first dozen or so rows of seats were packed, the tone in the auditorium seemed subdued. Carlos scanned the audience for familiar faces. Some of the kids he recognized from high school, others from around town. He spotted a pretty girl with fluffy blond hair sitting on the aisle toward the back of the crowd. She had hung out at Rainbow Dance over the summer, during teen dance nights at the school. What was her name? Reilly? Kelly?

Something Irish like that. She looked like a ballet dancer and probably studied here. Then he remembered. Daly. Daly Flanagan. She dated Ray Catelano, who also danced at the Academy and had his car fixed at Carlos's dad's shop.

Carlos started down the aisle toward her, happy to see a familiar face, wondering where Ray was. But as he approached Daly, a dark-haired girl slipped into the last empty seat in the row. She had a long, graceful neck, and her skin was pale against the chocolately brown of her thin-strapped T-shirt. When she turned to talk to Daly, Carlos caught his breath. The girl was simply beautiful, with delicate features and enormous eyes. As she spoke with Daly, her whole face, her whole body seemed to radiate incredible energy and life. How come he'd never seen her around before? She had the poise, carriage, and elegance of a real ballerina, though she looked as though she was about his age. Even in a school as big as Lincoln High he would have spotted someone with her style. Of course, he had never seen Daly before this summer, either. Advanced Academy students had quirky academic schedules at Lincoln.

Before he could give the girl another thought, Peter MacGregor was at the podium calling the meeting to order.

Carlos quickly sat down, a couple of rows behind the girls. He leaned forward attentively as Peter began speaking, laying out the problems of the school. But every few seconds Carlos's eyes drifted across the aisle and rested on the dark-haired girl. Would Daly remember him from the summer? Would she introduce him to her beautiful friend?

♡ ♡ ♡

" . . . So the problems have been building for a long time," Peter MacGregor informed the audience in a somber voice. He ticked off the points on his fingers. "Enrollment, even in the children's classes, our mainstay and our future, is down. Adult beginner classes had to be canceled the past two semesters because so few signed up. Meanwhile expenses have risen, and without High Falls Ballet Company performances to give us a public presence in the community, I only see our situation as getting worse. Those are the hard facts. . . . "

Sophy listened to the litany of the Academy's woes and fought not to put her hands over her ears.

"This isn't making me feel better," Daly confided in an undertone.

Sophy nodded in agreement as Peter summed up his comments, "So any—no, *every*—suggestion will be appreciated. All of us on this stage, board members included, would do almost anything—"

"Anything legal, he means!" Sophy's mother interjected from the front row where she sat with Daly's mom and some of the other parents.

Peter's careworn face lit up with a charming smile, and for a moment Sophy glimpsed the handsome young premier danseur he had been twenty years ago, the same star who graced the poster above her desk.

"Considering we have a lawyer on the board here, and a few in the audience, I'd better agree with Mrs. Bartlett's comment, at least in public," he joked. "But, seriously, folks. Every and any suggestion would be appreciated."

Hands flew up. Sophy worked up her courage as one by one, suggestions from the audience were batted down. An aggressive ad campaign to promote the school and spark new interest was too expensive. Rounding up a couple of famous dancers, then using the senior students from the school to put on a *Nutcracker*, sounded good. But facts about declining box office sales over the past few years doused that idea. Sophy swallowed hard, then jumped up.

"Sophy!" Peter called her name warmly from the podium.

Sophy cleared her throat. She never had trouble dancing in front of an audience, but speaking in public was a new experience. "Umm—" she began to stammer. The she remembered that her whole future, the future of the Academy, was on the line. "When I was in New York this summer, I heard people talking about a school that saved itself by renting space to classes in the theater department of a local university. Maybe some of the dance classes at High Falls University might need to use our space. I know continuing ed, where my mother teaches, sometimes needs more class space," she finished, and caught her mother's eye.

Her mother looked proud of her. Heartened by her support, Sophy sat down, and the room buzzed with conversation.

Peter conferred with some of the others onstage, then brought the meeting back to order. "Good idea, Sophy. In fact, it's one we've thought of but haven't really pursued. I'm not sure the university is in good enough shape to afford rentals. Still, it is possible." As Peter stopped to make a note, a voice spoke up from behind Sophy.

"Excuse me, but I think I have an even better idea."

Peter peered into the back of the audience. Sophy turned around, feeling a little annoyed. The first thing she noticed about the boy standing in the row behind her was his incredible posture. The second thing was his arrogance. "Who's *that?*" she murmured.

As if to answer her, he announced to the crowd, "My name's Carlos Vargas, and I'm from Rainbow Dance."

"Oh, Carlos," Peter said, nodding at the boy with a familiarity that surprised Sophy. She had vaguely heard of Rainbow Dance, some ballroom and folk dancing center downtown, near the bus depot. What was a guy from that place doing here? "So what's your take on all this?" Peter invited Carlos to continue.

"I think that—Sophy's?" He hesitated and smiled in Sophy's direction. She kept her expression neutral, but nodded to acknowledge her name. "Sophy's idea is good, but it's only a temporary solution. Or it could be. Some semesters the university will need space; some it won't. From what Peter said, it sounds like the Academy's problems are ongoing. But what if Sophy's idea could be made more permanent?"

"How?" Daly asked aloud.

"Just like you guys, Rainbow Dance has problems. Different ones, though," Carlos continued. "We're in a tiny space, but our enrollment isn't dropping. It's growing like crazy. You've seen, Daly. You've been there."

"Yeah!" Daly said with a smile. "It's wild!"

"When were you there?" Sophy whispered. She couldn't believe Daly actually knew this guy.

Before Daly could explain, Carlos whatever-his-name-was went on. "So I'm not speaking for Rainbow Dance. Just for myself. This is my idea," he added, sounding to Sophy more than a little arrogant. "Since we need space and have money, and you have space and don't have money, the two schools could join forces. Become partners."

"Partners?" The word echoed through the audience. But it was Sophy who jumped up and spoke before Peter or anyone else could say anything. "You mean you want us—a nationally renowned ballet school—to team up with a ballroom dancing business? Like, you have to be kidding! What do you people know about ballet?" she charged.

"What do you know about ballroom?" Carlos shot back, his dark eyes narrowing.

"Not much, and I intend to keep it that way!" Sophy countered. "This is a serious ballet school. Our dancers go on to major ballet careers."

"Well, some of our dancers *are* major on the ballroom circuit," he retorted, his voice rising. "One of our instructors was two-time National Ballroom Champion. . . ."

Whatever that might be! Sophy thought. "That kind of connection will ruin the reputation of this school, and everyone here knows it!" she said. She turned toward the stage, expecting Peter to support her.

Sophy's eyes widened as she realized that Peter was stroking his chin thoughtfully. "You know," he said, "that may not be a bad idea."

"What?" Sophy said, outraged. She hated what Carlos was suggesting. Everyone who was serious about ballet at the Academy should hate it as much as she did.

Frustrated, she whirled back to face Carlos, but found herself too flustered to speak. *This guy's a hunk!* The words actually crossed her mind. For the first time in her life Sophy found it hard to look a guy in the eyes—an incredibly handsome guy. Jet-black short hair, one small earring, a straight nose, and dramatically high cheekbones. And that posture! She couldn't get over the pride with which he carried himself. She was used to being around male dancers, but none of them looked quite like Carlos. Suddenly Sophy's face went red. What was she thinking of? *Forget it, girl!* she admonished herself. Without another word to Carlos she turned her back on him and sat down, grateful that other voices were taking up her argument.

"Sophy's right!" Shanti Patel called out from where she sat up front with her parents.

"But what a great way to save the Academy!" Laverne Grey said from across the aisle. "We'd still have a place to study, plus a chance to check out other kinds of dance classes."

The argument continued. Some students agreed loudly with Sophy; some parents, too. Others applauded Carlos. Finally, Peter took charge of the floor.

"I know the owners of Rainbow Dance," he said. "The Ivanovs are a very interesting couple. Both of them have extensive experience with various forms of dance. Teaming up with their school might actually bring a good, creative boost to both our student bodies. Laverne made a good point there. On the other hand, a merger would be very big step for both schools. I'll phone the Ivanovs after this meeting. Now could I have some volunteers for a committee to study the possibility of joining the schools?"

"Mr. MacGregor?" Carlos spoke up once again.

"Now what?" Sophy grumbled and, frowning, turned around. Carlos smiled in her direction.

Though he kept his voice loud and addressed the audience, Sophy felt he was talking only to her.

"I'd just like to invite people here to check out Rainbow Dance. To see what we're about. Tomorrow night, Friday, we have our open-dance night. It's only five bucks for people who don't take classes at the school. We've even got a special studio for teens. It's lots of fun, really."

Sophy thought that was a terrible idea. She glared at Carlos, but he smiled back, anyway. She turned around and stared at her sandals. Carlos's frank gaze unnerved her, and that made her mad. If he thought charm would change her mind about ballroom dancing, he had a lot to learn about Sophy Bartlett.

"If this crazy idea goes through, that's the end of the Academy," she declared hotly to Daly.

Daly shook her head. "Don't jump to conclusions, Soph. He's got a point. A merger just might work. Besides, it might be fun, add some life to this place."

"I can't believe you're saying this!" Sophy gasped.

Daly grinned. "Stop looking at me like I just sprouted another head! Rainbow Dance is a pretty cool place."

"How would you know?" Sophy asked.

"I've been there—"

"When?"

"Over the summer, while you were away in New

York," Daly said matter-of-factly. "Like I wrote you. One hot and boring July night, the Flanagan tribe decided to check it out. I went with Sean and Shannon and their significants of the moment," Daly said, referring to her older brother and sister. "The open-dance session on Fridays is to die for. We danced all night until we could barely stand. You'd love it."

"No way." Sophy felt betrayed. "Why didn't you tell me about this before?"

"Didn't you read my letters?" Now Daly sounded hurt.

Sophy winced. "Sure. But I skipped everything except stuff about the Company and school. Gossip like that."

Daly laughed good-naturedly. "It figures. But not to worry. Let's all go tomorrow night. There's supposed to be some tango demonstration. Besides, I'm always up for dancing salsa, and Ray's into the swing thing. We can round up some of the guys from class. P. J. and some of the other kids love that place."

P. J., Sophie's very own partner from the Academy, hung out at Rainbow Dance? What, Sophy wondered, had happened to all her friends over the summer? Had they all lost their minds? Ballet dancers did *not* hang out at ballroom schools.

"So you'll come with us tomorrow?" Daly asked as the meeting broke up.

"Over my dead body," Sophy replied. She gathered her bag and marched out of the auditorium.

She walked into the hallway and felt herself getting furious all over again. That Carlos person was holding court. A group of parents and her own friends were gathered around him, all talking excitedly. She held her head high, suddenly conscious of her own posture.

Their eyes met for a second. "Sophy, wait," Carlos called out. "I want to talk to you."

Sophy raised her head even higher and breezed right by, not even giving him a second look.

♡ ♡ ♡

"This looks more like party central than a dance school!" Sophy exclaimed Friday night. Sophy, Daly, and Ray had just paid admission to Rainbow Dance's weekly open-practice session.

The receptionist stamped their hands. "Under-twenty-ones in studio three, the last room down the hall. Sodas and snacks on the house."

Holding Daly's hand, Ray led the way to the studio. Sophy trailed behind, wending her way through the crowd. The people thronging the hall and adjacent studios ranged in age from kids like her to couples her grandparents' generation. Spirits were high. Everyone looked like they were up for a good time.

"Admit it, Soph!" Daly prodded. "You're glad I dragged you here."

"Too soon to tell." Sophy was not ready to concede that Daly was right. Rainbow Dance did look like a very happening spot. Though what was happening here didn't even remotely relate to ballet.

"Since when does Sophy Bartlett turn down a good time?" Ray Catelano laughed, stopping to slick back his dark hair in front of a mirror. Ray was dressed in his grandfather's vintage zoot suit and looked up for some hot swing dancing.

"Ever since she came back from Summerdance in New York. I had to drag her kicking and screaming out of the house tonight," Daly teased. "Ballerinas don't party!" she mocked.

Sophy reached forward and pretended to strangle her friend. "We partied lots in New York. We just didn't call dance parties dance *classes*."

"But you can see why Carlos said they needed more space. Ballroom's big," Daly told her as they squeezed through the crowd. "Physically, this place is too small."

"True." Sophy couldn't believe the school's cramped quarters. There were only three modest-sized studios lining the hall, and one bigger room at the end. Everything smelled of curry from Patel's take-out joint downstairs, and the place was stifling. She peeled off her short cotton cardigan and smoothed her clingy tee over the waist of her miniskirt. "I can't believe they don't have air-conditioning."

"Sophy, this way!" Daly called, reaching back for her hand. She led Sophy through a pair of open double doors into a wall of salsa music. Lights were down. Couples moved gracefully to the complex Latin beat.

Sophy began to grin. The scene reminded her of

moving as one   43

the closing night party at the summer workshop in New York. "This I could get into!" she shouted at Daly.

Daly gave her the high sign just as Ray tugged Daly onto the floor. "Do you mind?" Daly hesitated, calling back over her shoulder.

Sophy shook her head no. P. J. was supposed to turn up a little later with some of his friends from the university. She could dance with him. Meanwhile, Sophy was content just to watch couples dance. She had to admit some of the dancers looked really good. She couldn't believe how smoothly they moved together. The only time she'd been in a room full of salsa dancers they had all been ballet students, and Empire State Ballet Company dancers. This was different. The kids here danced with a tighter, sexier style.

If only the room weren't so hot. Sophy lifted her thick hair off the back of her neck. Even standing still she was beginning to sweat. Where were those free refreshments? Sophy scanned the dance floor. She recognized kids from Lincoln High: Johnny Mays, from her junior homeroom. Kristy Evans. And some guy from lit class was dancing with Shanti. Johnny waved her over. Sophy waved back. A cold drink first. Then she'd join them.

She finally spotted the refreshment table by the fire exit. The door was propped open for ventilation. And standing right next to the door . . . Sophy's good mood soured.

Carlos Vargas. Of course. Had she actually thought he'd invite the whole Academy to open-dance night and not turn up himself?

Weird she hadn't spotted him sooner. He positively oozed self-confidence, arrogance, and pride. A real Mr. Ego. Whatever, he certainly stood out in a crowd. Sophy couldn't say the same for the girl with him. She was sallow, small, and faded into the woodwork.

Not the type I'd imagine him with, she thought. Though why she should bother thinking anything about anybody connected with Carlos was beyond her.

♡   ♡   ♡

"*She's* got to be from the Academy," Inez declared, standing on tiptoe, trying to get a better look at the girl standing in the doorway. The girl was positively eye-catching, Inez's fantasy of a real ballerina.

She wore a skimpy silvery-gray T-shirt, a dark miniskirt, and a pair of straight-out-of-*Vogue* high platform sandals. As she lifted her shiny auburn hair off her neck, she looked around, as if trying to find someone, or something. Inez instantly envied her straight, aristocratic nose. Touching her own turned-up nose, Inez sighed. She watched as the girl drifted farther into the room. She moved with a deliberate grace, as if she were crossing a stage. Then the music stopped, dancers milled around, and the crowd just seemed to swallow her up. Turning to Carlos, Inez sighed. "To look—to move like that!"

"Like what?" Carlos asked, following Inez's

gaze. He was tall enough to see over the crowd. Inez watched as his face fell. "Oh, *her.*"

"You know her?"

Carlos lifted his shoulders. "Sort of. Her name's Sophy." He paused and tilted his nose in the air and mimicked an English accent. "Sophia Stuck-up."

"She's English?" Inez asked.

"Nope. Just thinks she's better than anyone else. The princess type."

Inez giggled, but was disappointed. "She's that bad?"

"Worse. She was at the meeting last night. Let's say the word 'snob' fails to define her." Carlos continued to look in Sophy's direction. Inez watched him taking Sophy in. "Too bad," he said half to himself. Then he added in a louder, careless tone, "She thought I was one-upping her at the meeting—that's *her* problem. After all, it's *her* school that's closing."

Inez felt a wave of sympathy for Sophy. "I'd feel rotten, too. The Academy's a pretty famous school. She looks like she was born to be a ballerina." She also looked a little lonely, Inez suddenly realized.

"Whatever . . ." Carlos's expression hardened. "If the merger goes through, she's going to be a real downer about it. She's really against the whole thing. And kids at the Academy will probably listen to her. I got the impression she's some sort of leader there."

"Like you, here," Inez pointed out. "Admit it, Carlos. You love hogging the spotlight."

"More like I love being in charge," Carlos admitted cheerfully. "Unfortunately, she does, too."

"Figures." Inez fiddled with the neckline of her brightly embroidered blouse. "Carlitos, wouldn't it be better to have her on your side? If the schools merge, it'd be better if people could have fun working together, not be at each other's throats all the time." Inez caught sight of Sophy again. Fragile and delicate, like a ballerina. And, like a ballerina, really really strong underneath. Whatever she was, she was beautiful, a real traffic stopper, and something about her eyes . . .

Inez decided Carlos was wrong about her. "She *looks* like a pretty nice person," she said.

"Looks can be deceiving." He paused, before adding, "She's so above it all, she thinks ballroom dancing and people like us aren't worth the time of day."

"Does she now?" Inez remarked as a faster salsa tune blasted out of the speakers. "Well, why don't you show her different?"

Carlos just stared at Inez a second, then slowly began to smile. He smoothed his hair, tugged down his sleeves, and crossed the dance floor.

Chapter Four

One song ended, another began. Sophy breathed a sigh of relief as Daly and Ray approached, holding three sodas. She could avoid the refreshment table now, and Carlos.

"So what do you think, Sophy?" Ray asked, handing Sophy a soda. She held the icy can against her face before opening it. As long as Carlos stayed on his side of the room, and she on hers, she could deal with this scene. "Isn't this place really cool?" he remarked

"Hot's more like it!" Daly punned, pulling a colorful handkerchief out of Ray's pocket and mopping her brow.

"Daly's got a point," Sophy admitted, hazarding a glance at the refreshment table. The mousy girl was still by the door, talking to a group of guys. Carlos wasn't one of them. Carlos, Sophy realized, had vanished. Maybe he was out on the fire escape catching some air. She relaxed a little and focused back on Ray. "Cool, hot, fun, whatever!" she said. "Rainbow Dance is just fine. But I can't really take all of this seriously. It's party stuff. Anyone with half a sense of rhythm and two feet can dance salsa."

"You have two feet, so I guess that means you'll give it a try!" The voice made Sophy whirl around.

Carlos was standing behind her. In her high-heeled platform shoes, Sophy stood almost five eight. He was taller, though a little shorter than he had seemed at the Academy auditorium. Up close he radiated an energy that Sophy found unnerving. He held out his hand. She just stared at it. "May I have this dance?" he asked with exaggerated formality.

Sophy tightened her grip on her soda can. "I'm—I'm waiting for P. J." Maybe he'd think she had a boyfriend and leave her alone.

"P. J.?" Daly spoke up. "I just saw him dancing with Elena. He'll be over later."

Sophy made a mental note to subject Daly to a slow, lingering death later that night.

"P. J.?" Carlos let his question hang.

"My partner. As in *dance* partner," Sophy spelled it out.

"Of course."

Of course? Of course what? Of course he isn't my boyfriend—like no way would a person like me would have one? Or of course I'd only know a guy who was a dance partner? Sophy felt vaguely insulted. She hadn't even allowed herself to think of guys in that way, yet. Ages ago, she had made up her mind to put all her energy into her dancing, not dating. Still, she liked to think that guys would at least *think* of asking her out.

The music changed again. This time the salsa tune was even hotter, true club style. Feeling angry, she looked up at Carlos. His face wore a formal sort of professional smile—the kind Sophy herself often wore onstage—the kind that hid her feelings. But his dark, heavy-lidded eyes held a challenge.

"Why not?" she tossed off, handing her soda to Daly. Brushing her hair off her face, she followed Carlos onto the dance floor. She could handle salsa and show him a thing or two while she was at it.

He took her right hand in his left, and put his right hand on her back. Waiting only an instant to catch the beat, he began to dance. Sophy was conscious of the light but firm touch of his hand on her back, guiding her into a series of complex turns. She liked salsa and had danced it before, but never like this. The place was crowded, and lots of guys there were good dancers. But no one there danced like Carlos. He seemed married to the music, to the floor, to the crowd, and to her own sense of rhythm and movement. She was astounded.

"You're incredible," she gasped.

"You're not bad . . . for a ballet dancer," he said.

Sophy tried to glare at him, but she couldn't. The music was too happy, and she recognized that Carlos was by far the best dancer on the floor. "Is that a compliment?" she finally retorted.

"Sort of," Carlos hedged. For a moment Sophy saw something flicker across his face, a look of respect, or intrigue. She couldn't tell which. "You *are* a born dancer. I didn't expect the ballet type to get so down and dirty like this!"

Sophy didn't know how to answer that. He couldn't admit right out she was good. But she couldn't tell if he was insulting or complimenting her. Or both. So she turned off her head and let her body feel the music. He led her through an intricate series of fast inside and outside turns. Sophy had to concentrate to keep up.

Out of the corner of her eye she watched other dancers, picking up little details of their movements, trying to copy the best girls' styles. Suddenly Sophy realized one girl was scrutinizing her as if she were some kind of dress on sale. The feeling was distinctly uncomfortable, and Sophy was glad when Carlos spun her around.

By the time Sophy saw the girl again, she was involved with her own partner, a slightly older guy whom Sophy took for a teacher. Sophy checked her out. The girl was a sexy, dynamite dancer, and moved with the same professional ease as Carlos. Sophy wondered if they knew each other. With her sloe eyes, dark hair, and exotic looks, she seemed older. She could have been in college or in her twenties; or maybe beneath her careful makeup, she was Sophy's age. She caught Sophy's glance and arched one finely shaped eyebrow, then looked seductively at her own partner and intensified her dance. Her short clingy red dress hugged every curve.

"Now that's sauce!" some guy said, pointing to the girl in the red dress.

Carlos turned. "Roxanna, of course," he said.

Sophy couldn't see his face, but he sounded a little proud.

Sophy tried to copy some of the girl's moves, but soon lost her to the crowd on the floor. So she threw herself into her own dancing, inspired by Carlos—or challenged. Whatever, he made her dance her best.

"Go, Carlos!" someone yelled. People snapped their fingers, stomped, clapped to the beat.

The song ended and applause broke out, but before Sophy could catch her breath, a different sort of music began. The tempo matched the steady rhythm of her heartbeat. The melody was hypnotic and cut right to Sophy's soul.

Carlos looked at her with new admiration. "You dance a pretty mean salsa, Miss Sophy Bartlett!"

Sophy smiled coolly back at him.

"Now let's see your tango."

"Tango?" Outside of cartoons, or Three Stooges movies, Sophy never had seen a tango danced.

Before Sophy could protest, Carlos's arm was around her back, his hand locked in her palm, pulling her so close, their chests touched. She could feel his warmth through the light fabric of his shirt, and her knees went wobbly. No guy ever had held her this way before. Dancing ballet pas de deux with P. J. never had felt like this. Sophy stiffened and tried to push away.

"Relax. This is called a tango hold," Carlos said in a cool, professional tone.

Sophy suddenly felt like a fool. Carlos wasn't

coming on to her. This was part of the dance.

"Listen to the music. Just follow," he instructed. Then again, waiting a moment for the right beat of the music, he began to move.

Follow what? Sophy wondered, then found the firm pressure of his hand on her back, the push of his other hand against her, guiding her this way, then that, moving smoothly to the insistent rhythm. Trying to follow him took all her concentration. The dance progressed around the room. Carlos guided Sophy so they didn't collide with other couples.

But in spite of his lead, Sophy kept tripping over her own feet. Then his. "Whoops. Sorry!" she said.

Carlos didn't respond, except to lead the dance out of the center of the floor, over toward the refreshment area. Until, with the music still playing, he stopped. Sophy found herself standing by the fire door, next to Carlos's sallow-faced friend.

Humiliated at not being able to finish the dance, Sophy tossed back her hair and folded her arms tightly across her chest. As if he read her thoughts, Carlos said, in a slightly condescending tone, "Tango's hard." He reached out and took the other girl's hand. The girl smiled shyly at Sophy. "Have you ever danced with a partner before?" Carlos asked Sophy.

"Yes. Like I told you. P. J. and I have been partners for a couple of years now."

"That's not the same thing. You've been partnered, but you've never danced *with* a partner. It's different. It's the heart of all social dancing," he explained. "It's about relationship. About leading and being led. About following."

Leading the other girl onto the floor, Carlos said over his shoulder, "Watch."

"This should be rich!" Sophy mumbled. She leaned back against the wall, catching the breeze from the open door, and watched skeptically as another tango melody began. Carlos pulled his new partner into the circle of his arms.

Like Cinderella! Sophy thought, her eyes widening. At Carlos's touch the girl blossomed. Her posture straightened. From the top of her dark head to the tip of her tee-strap heels, the girl's every cell seemed to come to life. Sophy gaped, spellbound as the couple traveled the room, locked in a passionate embrace. They matched so incredibly—as if they were made for each other. Sophy felt a twinge of— *of what, Bartlett?* She fought back the color rising to her face. She was actually jealous.

Who wouldn't be? she told herself. Of dancing like that. She didn't *want* to admit ballroom dancing could be an art, but watching Carlos and the girl glide across the floor with such intensity and grace—it was pure beauty. The way she felt when she danced a pas de deux except—

Sophy suddenly realized why she did feel jealous, sort of left out. It was as if they were dancing a secret.

Except it was a very public secret. Everyone in the room had stopped to watch the couple. Then the tango ended, and the room burst into applause.

Looking proud and happy, Carlos headed back, still holding the thin girl's hand.

The next tango started, and the girl with the red dress stepped between Carlos and his partner. "This one's for me!" she said, loud enough for Sophy to hear.

The thin girl just shrugged and walked over to stand beside Sophy as Carlos began dancing with his new partner. Suddenly as Sophy watched, something changed. The passion was no longer pretend. The new girl was stronger, bigger than Carlos's friend, and together she and Carlos covered incredible amounts of space on the floor. It was as if they were flying—but in slow motion, as if the floor were somehow holding on to them. The girl danced with a brash, in-your-face quality, and without the natural grace of Carlos's first partner. Still, Sophy had to admit she, too, was one of the best dancers she'd seen.

"Great together, aren't they?" a soft voice commented shyly.

Sophy wrenched her eyes off the dance floor. It was Carlos's first partner. "I guess so—I mean I've never seen tango before. They're incredible."

"That's why Nadia Ivanov paired them up. That's Roxanna. The Ivanovs—the people who run this school—she's their daughter." The thin girl flashed a warm smile and poked out her hand. "By the way, I'm Inez and you're—?"

"Sophy Bartlett." Sophy shook Inez's hand.

"Those two are great together, but you were, too. I think you're the better dancer," Sophy added frankly.

Inez looked incredulous. "Come off it. Who are you kidding? Roxanna's the star of ballroom around here—she's already preparing for the Olympics."

"Olympics?" Sophy repeated, horrified. "Ballroom dancing's going to be in the Olympics? Like skiing? Or wrestling?"

"Wrestling to music?" Inez giggled at Sophy's reaction. "I like that. But really, isn't it the best? Someone's finally figured out dance is really as demanding as any other sport."

"I guess—" Sophy conceded, feeling skeptical. She herself had great coordination, but hated most sports except for skating. They just didn't make her feel graceful and beautiful the way ballet did.

"Think ice dancing. Except this will be in the summer, like gymnastics," Inez suggested as Daly and Ray walked up.

"Hi, Inez," Daly greeted her. "Didn't realize you knew Carlos."

"Forever—" Inez groaned. "He's my brother."

"Your brother?" Sophy repeated, feeling a surge of relief. "Oh!" she said, suddenly confused at her feelings.

"One of three. I'm the only female Vargas, except for my mother, of course."

Sophy let her gaze travel from Inez to Carlos. She must have been blind not to see it. They had the same enormous black eyes, full lips, and beautiful smile. Inez was more delicate and poetic in her movements. Carlos, however, exuded incredible power and magnetism with every step he took.

Then who was Roxanna? Sophy wondered, turning her attention back to the dance floor.

"They're great, but you know," Sophy said after a moment watching the couple, "I liked the two of you together better. In some way you move more smoothly. More in unison."

"We'd better!" Inez said indignantly. "We've been dancing together for nearly eight years now. Ever since I was seven going on eight and he was ten. That's when the Ivanovs offered us both scholarships. But now"—Inez shrugged offhandedly— "judges know we are brother and sister. It shows. We just aren't as convincing at competitions. Ballroom is supposed to give the impression of romance. Like that—" She gestured to the dance floor, where Carlos and Roxanna were beginning another dance. As Sophy watched she wondered how Inez could sound so complacent about losing her partner.

As if reading her mind, Ray asked, "But who do you dance with now?"

"I'm still trying out partners," Inez answered. "I haven't found anyone right yet—rather, Mrs. Ivanov hasn't," she added tightly. "It's sort of up to her. At our age and our competition level, we still really represent the schools. If we become famous,

Rainbow Dance will, too. But becoming good enough to move on to the Nationals depends on who you can really dance with. It's a smallish scene, and to find the right person takes time. Right now I haven't got a regular partner."

Inez intrigued Sophy. The more she talked about ballroom, and Carlos, and the school, the less shy she seemed. Just then Carlos and Roxanna glided past them. Carlos winked at Inez over Roxanna's shoulder. Inez gave him the high sign, but Roxanna seemed lost in the dance.

"That romance isn't pretend!" Daly commented as the couple moved off.

Sophy nodded. "I can't believe that's all performance."

"Neither can—" Inez cut herself off. "Anyway, the point is, they're convincing. They've got the makings of a great partnership. Everyone says someday they'll be champions."

"How does that happen?" Ray asked.

Sophy listened as Inez explained the difference between amateur and professional ballroom dancers. And how most kids under twenty or so were on the amateur circuit, and how she and Carlos already had a string of gold medals in the local junior competitions.

The talk of competitions turned Sophy off. She knew of pretty big ballet competitions for students, for kids like her, but not for professional dancers. Competition in general she could understand, but great professional dancers didn't compete for medals or prizes. Imagine a row of judges at a performance of *Swan Lake* at the Metropolitan Opera House in New York!

"But every couple wants to become National Champions," Inez went on. "Then your career is made for the rest of your life. You can dance anywhere, start schools, coach, teach—and who knows what the Olympics will mean for the top dancers. Maybe dancers will be on cereal boxes," she quipped.

Everyone cracked up, but Sophy barely managed a smile. Her pleasure in watching Carlos tango had evaporated. She was horrified.

Great. Just great! Just what the Academy needed to bolster its image in the ballet world. Kids from her school, on a cornflakes box.

♡ ♡ ♡

The tango section of the evening was over. Some muscle-bound jock from the university had claimed Roxanna as a partner, and the room now rocked to a big-band swing tune. Sweaty and overheated, Carlos threaded his way through the dancers and, on a hunch, headed out the fire door. *Good guess, Vargas!* She was there, leaning against the fire escape, head thrown back to catch the breeze. Pink and green neon lights from the Patel's restaurant sign cast crazy patterns on her face.

He wiped away the beads of sweat gathered on his temple and cleared his throat. "Sophy!"

moving as one 59

At the sound of his voice, she turned.

"You vanished before the last tango," he said, leaning against the brick wall of the building. He stopped a moment. He was still breathing hard from the tango waltz that had closed the set.

He waited for her to say something. But finally he couldn't stand it. "So? Do you see? This is what I live to do. What I love more than anything!" He stepped a little closer and smiled into her incredible gray eyes.

"It looked like fun."

Her cool, polite smile doused his joy. "Fun?"

"Yes, fun. Like in having a good time. Party stuff. The kind of dancing anyone can do."

Sophy's offhanded shrug twisted inside him. "You think this is just party stuff?" He refused to believe she was serious. "You're putting me on. Right?"

"Wrong."

It was nearly midnight. A cool breeze wafted up from the riverfront. Sophy chafed her bare shoulders. Carlos's first impulse was to warm her up. His second was to tell her to get lost. "Who do you think you are?" he blurted, fuming.

"What?" Sophy's shoulders stiffened.

"You've just insulted everyone I know!"

"Insulted?" Sophy sounded clueless. "Who? How?"

Carlos pointed back inside. Couples were whirling and bouncing and stomping to a fast tempo swing tune. "All of them. Everyone who's in there having fun. Sure, *anyone* can dance socially. That's part of what ballroom's all about. People dancing together, hanging together. You act as if something's wrong with that."

Sophy averted her gaze. "I didn't mean it that way," she said, sounding a little flustered. Suddenly she looked up and put her hand on his arm.

He pulled away and glared at her.

She shrank back slightly, but held his glance. "Carlos, listen to me. You're a born dancer. So's Inez. Lots of people in that room have talent. I can see that. Especially your partner, Roxanna. But"— Sophy hesitated—"but most of them, including your partner, Roxanna, wouldn't make the cut in a professional dance company. Everyone's different shapes and sizes. Take Roxanna. She's gifted, but her build's all wrong."

Carlos couldn't believe his ears. "You're saying Roxanna Ivanov is fat?" Jealous, that was it. Sophy was jealous of Roxanna. Is that what this was all about? Carlos fought back a smile.

"Fat?" Sophy scoffed. "Any girl would kill to have her figure. She's great looking, but she wouldn't make it in a ballet company. Ballet has higher standards—"

"More like sicker standards. Every girl in a ballet company looks like a stick!" Carlos spat the words out, seeing Sophy in a new light. Suddenly she didn't look so beautiful.

Sophy recoiled as if he'd punched her. For a second Carlos wanted to take his words back.

"Sophy—I—"

"This is going nowhere," she interrupted icily. "Why argue? It's just crazy to think any good can come out of Rainbow Dance partnering up with the Academy. The schools are two different worlds." Sophy searched for the right image. "It's sort of like the Patels's curry joint downstairs, teaming up with Le Coq D'Or out on Boulevard."

"Meaning you and the Academy are the three-star French restaurant?"

"Whatever," Sophy tossed over her shoulder as she headed back into the studio. "It just won't work."

From the fire escape Carlos watched Sophy make a left back toward the refreshment table where her Academy friends were talking. He watched her slender body negotiate the crowd. What a stubborn, narrow-minded snob. A stubborn, narrow-minded, *beautiful* snob. He shook his head and shrugged her off. He had no time for this girl.

Carlos marched back into the studio and deliberately made a right turn. He wanted to distance himself from Sophy. She was a downer, and he hated down people. He began snapping his fingers to the upbeat tune. Spirits were high. The dancers spun wildly around him.

After a minute or two, Carlos spotted a girl from one of the on-site swing classes at the Lincoln

Middle School, where he sometimes filled in for one of the older Rainbow Dance instructors. The girl was chubby, with a big, warm smile and, as he recalled, a great sense of rhythm. Like half the girls in the seventh grade, she probably had a crush on him. Now what was her name? Melanie something or other. He walked up to her.

"May I have this dance?" he asked, following proper ballroom protocol.

"Wow," her round, pretty face lit up. "Man. I mean, sure."

He put his arm around her waist, and together they rocked back and forth triple time to the swing beat. She was a little short for him, but a super dancer. They traded grins, and Carlos let the happy music inspire him. Now this was more like it. Carlos hated fighting. Almost as much as he hated French food. "I much prefer curry," he mumbled half to himself. "More spice, more fire, more flavor."

"Whatever you say, Carlos," said Melanie, looking happy but a bit bewildered.

Carlos stared down at her, confused, then realized he'd been talking to himself out loud, and started to laugh.

Chapter Five

Mirrors should be outlawed! Daly concluded late that night. Wearing her blue Tweety Bird pj's, Daly checked her reflection in the basement mirror and felt like a blimp. She sucked in her tummy, examined her right profile, then her left, and finally heaved a huge sigh. Skipping dinner hadn't shrunk her down even a quarter of an inch.

"You know what I really love about Rainbow Dance?" she asked Sophy.

A muffled grunt emerged from the couch where Sophy was sitting, cocooned in a sleeping bag. She was hugging Sebastian, Daly's ancient one-eared teddy bear. Daly couldn't tell who looked more miserable: Sebastian or Sophy.

Daly decided she might as well answer her own question. "Well, I'll tell you what I love about that school. Ray and I figured it out this summer. People dance there just because it feels good. It's not such hard work. It's fun, as in F-U-N."

Barefoot, Daly curtsied to the mirror, then put her arms around a make-believe partner and waltzed across the cluttered basement, past her practice barre and her brothers' gym equipment and plunked herself down in a chair across from Sophy.

Daly hadn't seen Sophy so down since she'd lost the role of the Sugar Plum Fairy to Sally Sanmarco two years ago in the student production of *Nutcracker.*

What was the point of a sleep over if your best friend was about as talkative as a potted plant? And tonight Daly was truly desperate for a heart-to-heart. On top of the whole mess at the Academy, Daly had another problem: Ray. Maybe it wasn't exactly a *problem,* but she needed to talk to her best friend about it.

Her feelings for the guy were getting stronger. Lately things had heated up between them and were getting pretty physical. Daly was feeling pressured and confused. Was this love?

Determined to ignore Sophy's blues, Daly plunged ahead. "What really turned me on to Rainbow Dance were all those different shapes and sizes—of people, I mean!" she added, flopping down next to Sophy. "Wasn't it great? Even some of the chubby kids looked really hot dancing salsa—or didn't you notice?" She put her face very close to Sophy's. Daly pulled the corners of her lips down and gaped goofily up into Sophy's eyes. "Old rubber mouth has spoken!"

"Get off it!" Sophy grumbled, but she cracked a small smile, then shoved Sebastian at Daly.

Daly shoved him back, and soon the two girls were wrestling on the couch, in hysterics. Finally they both fell back giggling. Daly laughed until her sides hurt, and tears trickled down her cheeks.

Grinning from ear to ear, she sat up. "Knew it. Knew that somewhere deep inside that doom and gloom my old pal La Bartlett Pear still lurked!"

Sophy sat up and looked sheepish. "Sorry for being such a grouch. Things got kind of strange at Rainbow Dance toward the end. Sort of left me with a bad taste in my mouth."

"You *were* having one of your more pruny moments," Daly joked, twisting strands of her fine hair around her fingers. Softening her voice, she asked, "Ready to tell me what happened?"

"No."

"What did Carlos do now?" Daly prodded.

"Carlos?" Sophy shrugged but blushed as red as her nightshirt. She turned her back on Daly and fished in her bag. A moment later she emerged with a hairbrush and looked more her cool, collected self.

Ray was right! Daly thought, fighting back a smile. Romance was brewing. Ballroom and ballet were about to team up in more ways than one.

Sophy began yanking the brush through her tangled hair. "Let me!" Daly offered, pulling Sophy back onto the couch and sitting cross-legged behind her. Gently she eased the brush through the snarls until Sophy's hair shone like silk.

"Thanks, Daly," Sophy said. "That feels better. I can't seem to do anything right tonight," she murmured. When she looked up, her eyes were bright with tears. "Carlos yelled at me."

"*Carlos?* As in Vargas?" Daly was shocked. "He's usually such a nice guy."

"Well"—Sophy chewed her lip, then admitted in a small voice—"I probably deserved it. I guess I insulted him."

"More like insulted his tango!" Daly said, trying to lighten Sophy up. She looked positively tragic.

Sophy actually laughed. "That, too. Would you believe he actually thinks that all those people at Rainbow Dance are—or could be—as serious about dance as we are? That they work as hard. That how they look shouldn't matter—sure, all sorts of kids can dance well—but, Daly, you know how much looks and size count."

"Do I ever!" Daly exclaimed. Half her life seemed to be spent trying to keep herself thin enough to make the grade at the Academy. Jan MacGregor had been known to demote girls from the advanced classes if their weight went up more than five pounds. She'd actually kicked out Sandra Meehan when she'd come back from the summer ten pounds heavier last year.

Sandra had gotten so depressed, she'd eaten herself into a real weight problem and now was in some kind of counseling. Her mom, a real stage mother type, had tried to keep the whole thing under wraps, but word leaked out, and the school actually got some bad press in a local paper. It was all a big mess. "Makes me wish, sometimes, I could be a ballroom dancer. Most of them aren't as thin," Daly remarked wistfully.

"Daly, you're not overweight. Maybe two or three pounds, but that'll come off with more work," Sophy told her. Daly could hear the impatience in her voice. But Sophy didn't understand the weight thing—not really. Sophy had the opposite problem. She had trouble keeping her weight up to one hundred pounds. She ate like a demon, and calories melted right off of her. "Besides," Sophy said now, "I've seen some of those ballroom competitions on TV. Those women are thin, believe me, beneath all those fluffy costumes."

"You're probably right," Daly conceded, just to get away from the topic. Thinking about how all these years of dancing might add up to a fat zero because she couldn't stay thin enough, or perhaps she'd stayed too short, or grown too curvy, or had calves that were overly developed, made her stomach feel hollow. In fact, she realized now, she felt so hollow, she needed something to eat.

She jumped up and tugged down her nightshirt. "Hey, speaking of weight, I read we can eat light microwave popcorn by the bowlful and not put on a pound—"

"I thought the microwave was broken." Sophy looked over at a utility cart by the sliding French doors.

"Not the one in the kitchen."

Sophy started after Daly. "I'll help you."

"Better not," Daly told her. "The parents are having

some major late-night domestic type meeting over the kitchen table. I'll be back in a sec."

Barefoot, Daly bolted up the basement steps two and three at a time. At the top of the stairs she winced. Except for a night-light in the hall, and the sliver of light seeping from beneath the kitchen door, the house was dark. It was late. Everyone was sleeping, except for her parents. She tiptoed down the hall and cracked open the kitchen door.

Her parents both looked up at once. "Daly? You're still awake?" her mother asked.

"Sure, still gossiping!" Daly answered breezily, but looked hard at her mother. Bridget Flanagan's face looked puffy, and there were circles under her eyes. *She's worried,* Daly realized. It's probably the Academy. Her mother was on the committee investigating details of how to work the merger. Daly stifled her curiosity. Neither of her parents seemed to be in the mood to give her the inside scoop. "Okay if I microwave some popcorn?" she asked.

Her father cracked a tired smile. If anything he looked more freaked than her mom. Weird. Definitely weird, Daly thought.

"Sometimes, Daly, I wish you'd eat your dinner and not snack so much at night," her mother told her, pulling her chair closer to the table so Daly could reach into the cabinet. "You barely touched your food at supper, and now you're starving."

"It's just that I worked up a good appetite dancing salsa. Besides, Mom, popcorn's good." Daly tapped the label on the box. "Lots of fiber. This brand's low-fat. Doesn't count for much," Daly informed her as she threw out the cellophane wrapper and plopped the bag on the microwave turntable. She punched up the timer, then slung her arms around her father's neck and peered over his shoulders at piles of papers strewn across the Formica tabletop.

"You guys look as if it's tax time or something. Did I miss a few months here? Isn't it September, as in start of the new school year? Are you worried about my dance classes?" she added, the playfulness going out of her voice. "My scholarship and all that!" The glance her parents exchanged went by so fast, Daly thought she had imagined it.

"Not tax time, and I wouldn't worry just yet about dancing and scholarships. Besides, none of this, old Curious Cat, is any of your business!" He reached back and tickled Daly. She doubled over, giggling.

"Sssssshhh! You'll wake the whole troupe!" her mother warned as the bell for the microwave went off.

Daly dumped the popcorn into a big ceramic bowl, grabbed a couple of sodas, and headed back downstairs. Sophy had cleared space on the coffee table and was punching the remote, flipping through channels on TV. She looked more up, more herself. Daly grinned in relief.

"What's on?" Daly passed the popcorn to Sophy.

Sophy grabbed a fistful and scarfed it down. Daly took one kernel and slowly licked the salt off of it to make it last.

"Sumo wrestling." Flick. *"Return of Swamp Girl: Part Two."*

"Not!" Daly covered her eyes. "Hate that stuff."

"Always The Weather Channel." Flick. "Or CNN?" Flick. An image of Fred Astaire and Ginger Rogers twirled across the screen. Sophy smiled wryly. "Seems I'm destined to be surrounded by frothy ballroom stuff tonight."

"Nothing's frothy about Fred Astaire. Jan MacGregor always says—"

Sophy broke in, mimicking her teacher's Scottish burr perfectly. *"He's one of the great natural dancers of our century, like Fonteyn. Who could argue that? Just look!"*

The two girls kicked back and watched a moment as the forties film stars waltzed through a glitzy production number.

"I wouldn't call anything in the under-twenty-one studio at Rainbow Dance 'frothy' tonight," Daly commented as a car commercial kicked in on the TV. "Carlos isn't frothy."

"Definitely not the word I'd use to describe him," Sophy agreed. "His dancing is strong, dramatic—"

"Ah, so he's not a completely bad guy."

"Bad guy?" Sophy tossed some popcorn at Daly. "Come off it. I never said that. He's just haughty, proud, and so sure of himself."

"Sounds a lot like someone else I know!" Daly said pointedly.

But Sophy barreled on, oblivious to Daly's jibe. "He actually thinks ballroom's as demanding as ballet. I just can't see why he wastes his talent on such fluff."

Daly considered that. She curled her toes up under the sleeping bag. "Beats me. I've never had a ballroom class. Might try it sometime, just to see."

"That'd be rich!" Sophy scoffed. "You could probably teach them all a thing or two."

"I don't know." Daly pictured Carlos dancing the tango first with Sophy, then with Inez, then with Roxanna on the dance floor. Sophy hadn't looked so great, though Daly would die before she'd tell her that. Instead, she said, "Carlos and his sister and Roxanna have studied ballroom as long as we've studied ballet. I bet it's harder to do right than it looks."

"Probably is," Sophy replied flatly. "But it's not as tough as what we do, every day, for hours in the ballet studio. And, believe me, when we audition for ballet companies, no one's going to give a shot to someone who comes from a ballroom school."

♡ ♡ ♡

Sophy stood in front of the fridge a few mornings later staring bleakly at the neat row of yogurt containers on the second shelf: all the flavors she usually loved. But today, like yesterday, and the day before, the thought of eating turned her stomach.

While the thought of a dance class before heading off to Lincoln High made her feet feel like concrete. She was supposed to be happy that the Academy was staying open on a week-to-week basis until the fate of the school was finally decided. But she wasn't. Every morning she felt like she was headed for a funeral.

Most sixteen-year-olds, she reflected now, don't have these problems. Most of the girls she knew, including Daly, were worried about clothes, and parties, boys or the lack of them; about falling in love, about a date for the Fall Swing Dance, about the sex thing.

Sophy was simply wondering how she'd live her life without the Academy.

"Life," she mumbled, slamming the fridge, "is the pits."

"Not to worry. Your only real problem, Sophy," diagnosed Emma Bartlett, "is you are simply not a morning person." The blond, blue-eyed eleven-year-old peered at Sophy over her glasses, downed another spoonful of cereal, then informed her, "Did you know Thomas Jefferson got out of bed every single day at dawn and poked his feet into a bucket of ice—"

"Would you just shut up!" Sophy moaned, definitely not up for one of her brainy sister's lectures. She poured milk into a mug to make hot chocolate. While she waited for it to heat in the microwave, she turned back to Emma, "Sticking my poor toes in an ice bucket won't help my dance career. Not that it matters now. Without the Academy, I've got no career. Besides which, I could care less about your Thomas Jefferson."

"You should," Emma insisted, pouring a second bowl of cereal. "Mr. Dougherty, my social studies teacher, says that trying to understand genius helps spur brain cell growth. Yours sure need something."

"Nothing's wrong with my brain cells," Sophy protested.

"Except they're all in your feet."

In spite of her blues, Sophy cracked up. "You're such a jerk!" she laughed, and affectionately whopped her sister with a towel.

"Now that sounds more like *my* Sophy!" her mother's voice broke in as she bounded down the last few steps of the side stairs and into the kitchen. After plopping a kiss on Emma's head, Anne Bartlett buttoned the sleeve of her silver-gray blouse and straightened the waistband of her slim, straight skirt. Like Sophy, her hair was a thick, reddish brown, and she was slender, small boned, and full of energy. But like Emma, she was a morning person.

She popped an English muffin into the toaster, then poured herself some coffee. She leaned back against the counter and grinned at Sophy. Her gray eyes positively glowed. "I've got some really great news!"

"About the Academy?"

Her mother nodded, and Sophy's heart soared. "So did the bank change its mind? Or did you guys on the committee find a corporate sponsor, or . . ."

Anne's laugh cut her off. "No. None of the above. But the merger with Rainbow Dance is almost a done deal. All that's needed now is a major fundraising campaign to finance physical renovations of the building. But the ballroom school will be able to bail the Academy out of debt for starters. The Ivanovs are thrilled."

Right. The Ivanovs. Carlos's partner's parents. "So then, that's that." Sophy felt like a lead weight had just dropped on her chest.

Anne's face registered surprise. "Don't you understand? The school's going to survive."

"No," Sophy stated. "Not *my* school. Not the Academy."

"It'll still be your school, no matter what they call it," Emma piped up. "I'm sure they'll keep you on scholarship. After your gig with Summerdance this summer you're a local star, Soph."

Sophy whirled around. "Butt out, Emma. You haven't a clue what's going on here. Who cares about a scholarship, or Summerdance, or anything—"

"Stop shouting at your sister," her mother warned. "Whatever has you ticked off, Sophy, don't take it out on Emma."

"Who's shouting?" Sophy remonstrated, then realized she was yelling so hard, her throat hurt. She sucked in her breath and pressed her hands to her temples. She fought to control her voice. "Look, Mom, whatever watered-down version of a dance school comes out of this, I don't want anything to do with it."

"Sophy, stop being so melodramatic. I swear, sometimes I think your talent is for acting, not dancing." In a softer tone she added, "Change is hard for everyone, Soph. But, think about it. You'll still have the same teachers, the same program of study at the new school. Most of the changes won't even affect you."

"Have you *been* to Rainbow Dance? Do you know what that place is like?" Sophy cried.

"All I know is that it's a thriving business and that Nadia Ivanov was a leading competitive dancer in the Soviet Union. Now hear me out," her mother ordered. "The Academy is simply expanding, and I think the expansion will be good. Everyone thinks the merger will revitalize the dance program in the long run—even the MacGregors, and you know what ballet purists they are."

"That's just a lot of hype to save the business," Sophy declared. "The MacGregors know as well as anyone a ballet-ballroom dance school can't possibly be taken seriously. But whatever they think, I don't care. I'm not going there."

Anne's expression hardened. "So is that it, Sophy? All these years of dance lessons and you give up? Just like that?"

"Give up?" Sophy gasped. "Oh, no. I'm not going to give up. I'm going to write Davidoff in New York. He said I should consider applying for their apprentice company. I'll just go there."

"Go to New York?" Emma and her mother cried at once.

"You'd leave home?" Emma looked horrified. "You'd leave us?"

"Not as long as I'm your mother and you're under eighteen," Anne declared firmly. "You're not leaving High Falls until after you graduate. That's two more years of school here, Sophia Bartlett. Whether you decide to continue at the Academy or not."

"But, Mom," Sophy pleaded, her voice breaking, "I can finish high school in New York. They have these special performing arts schools, just for people like me, who would be dancing with a company. The education's good, and . . . "

"And nothing. I won't hear of it. As it is, with me watching over your shoulder, you hardly study, you seldom get homework done. You're barely making the grade. All because your head is so filled with dance. If you quit regular school now, you'll ruin your life. I won't let that happen. Not to you." Anne Bartlett's face was pale, and her bottom lip was trembling. "Maybe I've indulged this dance thing too long. I should have listened to my instincts and never let you take that first dance lesson. I should have seen this coming."

"Seen what coming? That one day I'd be good

moving as one   77

enough to make a name for myself?" Sophy stared at her mother, and suddenly something made sense. "No, that's not it. Is it? You just don't want me to be good at something—something that, in spite of all your college degrees, you just can't understand."

Sophy stomped over to the dishwasher and yanked open the door. She jammed her mug on the top shelf. Her heart was pounding, and she wanted to scream. But when she faced her mother, her expression was hard, her voice cold. "You know, Mother, I think I just figured the whole thing out. You can't understand anything or anyone who's different from you. I bet that's exactly why Dad left you. You're so uptight and narrow-minded. I also bet that if he were here he'd take my side on this one. He'd let me go to New York." Sophy fairly spat the last words.

Anne turned white.

"What's Daddy got to do with this?" Emma cried, stricken.

"Ask her," Sophy challenged, holding her mother's gaze. "It's the big secret we're not supposed to talk about. All I know is that if he were here, things would be different."

Anne turned away from Sophy, meeting Emma's tear-filled eyes. "Your father has nothing to do with this. Nothing, Em," she said, but something in her voice told Sophy she was lying.

Sophy couldn't believe it. After all these years, she had somehow hit the mark. Her heart leaped up into her throat. "I'm right, aren't I? Daddy left you because—" Because why? Sophy knew she had almost guessed something, but what? What? She searched her mother's face. It was livid, but her eyes were full of pain. Suddenly Sophy felt terrible.

Her mother moved to put a protective arm around Emma. "What was between your father and me was just that, between us. It was a long time ago, and it has nothing to do with you"—Anne turned to Sophy, adding firmly—"either of you."

Emma looked from her mother to Sophy, then burst into tears. Without a word, she pushed back her chair and raced from the room.

Sophy was at a loss for words. She felt guilty, and horrible, and grim.

Her face set, her lips pursed, Anne Bartlett started to clear the breakfast things as if nothing had happened.

Sophy sank slowly into a kitchen chair. She hugged her arms to her chest, as if she could squeeze all her feelings back in. She was afraid if she moved, if she met her mother's eyes, she'd start crying so hard, she'd never stop.

Anne rinsed her hands at the sink, then reached for her suit jacket. As she started for the hall, she turned toward Sophy. Sophy braced herself and stared at the linoleum floor. She felt angry and hurt, but mostly disgusted with herself. She hated hurting Emma. She hated making her mother look so sad.

"Sophy," she said, her voice strained and tight, "I

know you're upset. I don't blame you. And things—well, I know you want to know about your father." She paused. "Look at me." She put her hand under Sophy's chin. Sophy looked up, but her eyes were blurred with tears. One spilled down her cheek. Her mother wiped it away with her thumb, then sat down beside her.

The tears kept coming—Sophy felt like she was suddenly crying for everything: the stuff at the Academy, her fight with Carlos, and now this about her father. Anne soothed her back in silence until Sophy's sobs quieted. Finally Sophy wiped away her tears and looked over at her mother. "I just don't understand—any of it," she said hoarsely.

"I wish I had the answers, Soph. Your father—well, he left. He just left. I don't know why things didn't work out, exactly." For a moment her mother hesitated. Sophy saw a look of pain cross her face before she went on. "You know how that is. Sometimes people fall out of love. Things don't click anymore. One day he was here; the next he was gone. Maybe I was to blame, but I honestly don't know why. Then the checks started coming—money orders, really, so I couldn't trace them. He took his responsibility to you kids seriously—even though he never had much money before he left, and I can't picture him rich now. But he's never abandoned you girls that way."

"Why didn't you try to find him?" Sophy asked.

She'd been so young when her father had left, it was all just a painful blur. She couldn't remember much about her mother then except she'd cried every time Sophy had asked about her dad. Sophy had hated the tears, so she'd just stopped asking.

"I—I . . ." Again her mother hesitated, then shrugged. "Whatever—that was a long time ago. At one point after he left I knew I just had to get on with my life. I had to put it behind me."

"How?" Sophy cried. "How can you just put it behind you? How can you live not knowing everything? What he was thinking, doing?" Sophy would have searched to the ends of the earth to find him, somehow. Just to ask why. "I don't understand."

"I know, hon. But, someday, maybe you will." Anne stood up, dried her own eyes, and looked down at Sophy. "I'd better see to Emma. She needed to cry herself out a bit before I went to her. She's like that."

Sophy knew what her mother meant. Emma was an odd kid. She had a very scientific way about her, and hated lately being what she called "babied."

"But before I go up there, I need to say one more thing about the Academy."

Sophy stiffened.

"Just listen," her mother pleaded. "I understand you don't like it. But the merger *is* going to happen. It's your school, Sophy, and if you want it to work, you'd better get behind this thing. Or have you come up with something better?"

Sophy heaved a sigh. "No," she admitted. "I said whatever I had to say at that meeting."

"Okay, then. I think you'd better sit down and do some serious thinking. If all or most of the Academy students feel like you and drop out, there's going to be no school. But if you're serious about dancing, you're going to have to get behind the merger, heart and soul. I was serious about the fund-raising part. And the students had better get busy on that right away."

"I guess," Sophy conceded.

"That's not good enough," her mother pointed out. "And half-baked enthusiasm isn't good enough for the Sophy Bartlett I've known since before she was born. What happened to the girl who single-handedly organized that dance performance to raise money for Donnie Paulson's hospital bills after that dirt-bike accident when you were in the sixth grade? Think about it," she said over her shoulder as she started up the stairs toward Emma's room.

Sophy pressed her hands over her eyes. What was she supposed to do? Throw herself heart and soul into something she didn't believe in?

"No," she wept. Her mother was wrong. This wasn't at all like Donnie Paulson.

Chapter Six

♡ "School spirit. I like that in people!" Roxanna declared, her voice dripping with sarcasm. She checked her watch and gloated. Students from the two schools were holding a meeting at Under Wraps, a wrap and enchilada food bar near High Falls University campus. So far, only kids from Rainbow Dance had showed. They had claimed three of the wrought-iron tables on the deck of the restaurant. The September sky was blue, the air was mild, and Roxanna, who hated damp cold days, was in her element. "Those Academy kids talk the big talk, but they don't seem to care what happens to *their* school."

Carlos stopped his pacing just long enough to scowl at her. "Give it a break, would you?"

"Don't take your frustrations out on me, Carlos," Roxanna said sweetly. "I'm here. Those Academy snobs obviously have stood us up!"

Which suited Roxanna Ivanov perfectly. After all, it was *her* parents who were bailing out that dumb Ballet Academy. So she should enjoy some special privileges at the new school—she couldn't quite picture what—maybe a private dressing room; there *was* all that space. The Ballet Academy, with its dwindling admissions, must have positively rattled around in that big old warehouse. Maybe she'd get leading roles, but in what?

Actually that Sophy person Carlos was so hooked on was right about one thing: It was hard, even for Roxanna, who considered herself blessed with an extravagantly wild imagination, to envision how combining the two schools would work. Would they share some classes, or just space? Roxanna hated ballet with a passion—mainly because she looked and felt all wrong dancing it. She was made for tangos, with high heels, and slinky black dresses that showed off her every curve—not tutus and pointe shoes.

But she could worry about that some other time. Today's first order of business was securing her position among the students from both schools. The meeting was being held in neutral territory, but Roxanna had taken charge and wanted to be sure in the new scheme of things she was leader of the pack. Now Roxanna lifted her face to the sun, closed her eyes, and said, "Oh, Purr! This makes me feel like a cat."

"And sound like one, too!" remarked Inez, just loud enough for Roxanna to hear.

"What's that, little sister?" Roxanna's eyes popped open, and she glared at Inez.

"Why, nothing!" Inez looked all innocent. But Carlos leaned against the railing of the deck and seemed annoyed. Out of the corner of her eye

Roxanna saw him check the big clock in the university bell tower and frown.

"I can't believe they'd cop out on us like this," he murmured, pacing from one side of the deck to the other, then back again.

"What?" Roxanna feigned surprise. "I thought that Katrina or Laura or whatever that little would-be ballet star with the red hair is called—"

"Sophy," Carlos and Inez snapped at once. Of course he'd never forget her name. Roxanna stored away that bit of information. Sophy Bartlett. She had made it her business to find out exactly who Carlos had been dancing with the other night. Especially when she had seen him trail her like a puppy dog right out to the fire escape. At least whatever happened out there had seemingly put both of them in a terrible mood.

Still, the girl spelled trouble, and Roxanna was determined to steer Carlos clear of her.

"Ah—right—Miss Sophy. She's the one who's so against the merger. Everyone is talking about it. She hates it. She's probably convinced her snobbish pals to skip this meeting." Roxanna lifted her shoulders.

"Don't be such a downer," Carlos turned on Roxanna. She felt like he had slapped her. But outwardly she smiled benignly.

"Who's being a downer? We're all here. It's their loss. We'll just make our plans without them. Right?" Roxanna looked around the small group gathered on the patio of the restaurant.

"We'll wait awhile longer," Carlos declared firmly.

One guy shrugged. "Sort of seems pointless to meet without them."

"No, we'll just make the plans for ourselves. They'll have to live with whatever we decide. That's only fair," Roxanna insisted.

"Besides, I wouldn't write them off just yet," Inez spoke up, clapping her hands together. "Here's Daly now. Look. Sophy Bartlett's with her."

"Knew Sophy would make it!" Carlos's smile broke Roxanna's heart.

"Can't say she looks thrilled to be here," Roxanna commented, but stood up and graciously waved the two girls over.

"Sorry we're late." Daly tossed her dance bag on the ground and flopped into a chair. Sophy took off her red backpack and sat beside Daly. Roxanna couldn't believe it: The girl actually sat with her nose in the air. "We missed the bus," she explained in a cool, precise voice, then looked around. "Where is everybody?"

"*We*'re all here!" Roxanna said, taking her first good look at Sophy by daylight. The girl was a knockout. But she held herself as if she were Princess Di. An auburn-headed ice princess. And her beige linen pants and sleeveless shirt looked straight from Fifth Avenue, not the local WalMart. Not just a snob. But rich. Figures. "I guess then it's just you two representing the Academy."

"No way!" Laverne Grey gasped, jogging up and

pointing out to the street where a tall, blond guy was parking an old van covered with colorful painted landscapes. The willowy black girl collapsed in the nearest chair and dusted off her jeans. "P. J. and the rest of us were clearing out one of the big studios on the ground floor. My dad's been using it for prop and costume storage, but some designers were coming in to draw up plans over the weekend for the renovation. Anyway, next thing we knew we were too late to even walk over here."

"Laverne's dad is a choreographer and teaches at the school," Daly informed the Rainbow Dance kids.

"Yeah," Laverne added. "He wanted to get some stuff done before he leaves town next week to work with a modern dance troupe out on the West Coast."

"So what's happening?" P. J. said, bringing over sodas from the take-out counter. He moved with a natural grace and was Roxanna's idea of the perfect male ballet dancer. But he couldn't hold a candle to Carlos. P. J. caught her eye and smiled, but he sat down next to Sophy. "Have we missed much?" he asked Sophy chummily, and popped open a soda for her.

Roxanna made a mental note to find out if they were dating.

"We just got here ourselves," Sophy said flatly. "Daly and I had to go down to Lincoln Middle School for a dance demonstration. It ran over."

"Hey, we also go there sometimes—Rainbow Dance is involved in that 'Dance in the Schools' program, too," Carlos said. He slicked back his hair, pulled up a chair right opposite Sophy, and straddled it.

Roxanna planted herself right next to him. Propping one hip against the deck rail, she cleared her throat and broke in. "We were waiting for you guys to start the meeting. Some of us have to get back to classes early this evening. Rainbow Dance runs on a nighttime schedule."

"True," Carlos said, then before Roxanna could open her mouth again, he jumped up, stuffed his hands in the pockets of his baggy jeans, and grinned at the gathering. "This is awesome. It's really happening. The schools are joining, and everyone turned up. Do we all know each other?"

Carlos began introducing people. It turned out Shanti Patel from the Academy was related to the Patels who ran the curry joint downstairs from Rainbow Dance. It was her uncle or something.

Susan Davis and Aiko Nakamura from Rainbow Dance both had kid sisters in the lower division of the Academy.

People marveled at how connected the schools already were. Roxanna bristled with impatience. "All this buddy-buddy stuff is nice and fun and there's lots of time for it later, but isn't it about time we got down to business?"

"Which is?" Ray asked. He had squeezed onto the same chair as Daly and had one arm around her to steady himself.

Roxanna opened her mouth to answer, but again Carlos took charge. "For starters, exactly what are we going to do to make this whole thing work?" Carlos looked right at Sophy when he said that. She met his glance, then deliberately shifted her gaze. Cool as ice, that one. Roxanna suddenly didn't trust her.

"I thought everything was worked out by the banks and people like that," Shanti commented.

"True," Carlos conceded. "But it's going to be *our* school, and we've got to be the ones to support the plan. Not just by talking but by doing something. By being proactive!"

"What's that?" Aiko asked.

"It means we take charge ourselves," Daly said. "My father's always talking about that at work. But how, Carlos? And what needs to be done, anyway?"

"Money," Roxanna said before Carlos got the chance. This was supposed to be her meeting, her chance to shine, and he was hogging the spotlight just to show off in front of that snobby ballet-Bartlett girl. "There's enough money for my parents to help the schools merge, but then that's it. The renovations are going to have to be major to make things work. Some local businesses are organizing a fund-raising drive." She paused to catch her breath.

"Right—and we should be part of it!" Carlos finished for her.

"Sounds like you two have it all figured out," Ray said wryly.

"No," Carlos and Roxanna declared in unison. There was a silence, then everyone started to laugh. Carlos was the first to speak again. "We are partners and tend to think alike—sometimes," he said, winking at Roxanna.

The wink set her heart racing, her head spinning, her blood right to her cheeks. Carlos went right on without skipping a beat. "So we have to organize our own fund-raiser."

"What kind of fund-raiser?" Shanti asked.

"That's a no-brainer. We're all dancers. We'll put on a dance performance," Laverne suggested. "But," she went on to warn, "it has to be something really special—outrageous, even—so we can get some good press. We've got to attract lots of attention."

"Outrageous?" Aiko repeated, her dark eyes bright. "Count me in!"

"Me too!" seconded Inez.

Roxanna looked around the group. The only person looking doubtful was that Sophy person. Sophy's reluctance inspired her; besides, she sort of liked Laverne. Laverne seemed to be the only Academy girl Roxanna had met so far who held promise. She looked like she knew how to have a good time, and wasn't so—well—innocent and uptight. She seemed like a real party animal, and Roxanna was a girl who loved to party.

"Laverne, you're a genius!" Roxanna complimented her with some genuine warmth. "I wish I had thought of that!" she added, feeling generous. Out of the corner of her eye she saw Sophy roll those big eyes and sink lower into her seat. Great! The girl hated it.

"The only question is: What kind of dance?" asked Daly. "Ballroom or ballet?"

♡   ♡   ♡

For a long moment Daly's question hung in the air.

Sophy held her breath. For her there was only one answer that mattered. One thing that could make everything right: Ballet all the way!

Then Carlos got up and shot a glance in her direction. She forced herself not to react, not to turn away, not to blush, to sit still as stone, though inside she was a jumble of feelings. She hadn't seen him since their exchange on the fire escape the other night. What must he think of her marching off like that, furious?

She knew what she thought of him: that he was arrogant, stubborn, and a regular Mr. Ego. She'd prefer if she never had to see him again.

Now she'd have to work with him. Of all the rotten luck.

"It's perfectly clear," Carlos announced, cocky as a crow. "We'll do both."

Sophy felt the breath whoosh right out of her, like the time she'd taken a bad fall in partnering class when P. J. hadn't caught her.

"Both?" Several voices echoed.

Sophy prayed she hadn't heard right. "Both?" she repeated, her mouth dry as sand.

"It's the only answer!" Carlos said, looking at her. He expected her to say something. She pursed her lips tighter and clenched her fingers around the armrest of her chair. Deliberately she turned away and fixed her gaze at the kids milling around the campus quad.

"Count me out," she murmured. "Like I'd be part of something that sounds straight out of Las Vegas." She hadn't meant for people to hear, not really. But Daly practically choked on her Coke. Ray doubled over laughing.

"Vegas?" Shanti repeated between giggles. "That's rare, really rare!"

Sophy hadn't meant to make a joke, but her mouth trembled into a smile. She shook back her hair and looked up—right into Carlos's face. He was standing over her, his expression puzzled, hurt, and downright mad.

Her cheeks grew hot. She sat up straighter and returned his stare.

"What's with you, anyway? Don't you want this thing to work?" he asked.

She shrugged. "Don't act so surprised. You know how I feel."

"Guess I do," he said, turning away. "I just thought you'd come to your senses, but now—"

But now? Now, what? Sophy suddenly could hear her mother's voice. Only yesterday morning she had tried to remind Sophy about the person she used to be. A leader. Someone who made things happen. Suddenly she wished she were another kind of person. The kind of person who could stop things from happening. She thought about Donnie Paulson. She thought about not having anyplace to take dance lessons. She thought about two more years of the MacGregors teaching, even though there'd be ballroom dancing in the next room, with loud practice sessions Friday nights.

When she looked up, Roxanna was examining her as if she were a bug. The girl was positively gloating. Why? What did Roxanna have against *her?* She barely knew the girl. Still, Sophy was not used to being gloated at. She decided she hated it.

"Carlos," she said, her voice weak at first. "Carlos," she repeated, standing up. Suddenly the murmur on the deck died down, and she was conscious of everyone looking at her. Sophy swallowed hard and forced herself to meet his eyes. He looked wary, and his jaw was set.

"I can't help how I feel about the school. I'm not thrilled. But—hey, it's the best deal we've all got. So whatever we come up with, I'll back it—heart and soul," she concluded, forcing herself not to mumble. She sat down and looked away. But not before she saw relief register in his face. *He cares!* she realized. For some reason her being onboard and backing this project really mattered to him.

"Way to go, Sophy!" Daly yelled.

"Now we're really cooking!" Ray said. Other kids cheered, and everyone began talking at once.

"Thanks, Sophy." Carlos's voice rose above the crowd. She looked up at the sound of it. He was looking at her carefully and sounded cautious. "Thanks for being honest."

"She's always that!" Daly piped up, and slung one arm around Sophy, one around Carlos.

Roxanna smiled coolly. "I'm glad you came around. Obviously Academy students listen to you." Something about her tone chilled Sophy right to the bone. She met Roxanna's dark eyes, but they were mysterious and hard to read.

"Still," Sophy admitted as the commotion died down, "I want this to work. But I don't want to embarrass myself or the school with some amateur performance. In the long run it won't do any of us— ballet or ballroom dancers—any good."

"Who has to be amateur?" Inez spoke up. "Carlos and Roxanna are pretty close to professional level right now. You look pretty professional yourself."

"For sure," Daly said, casting a proud glance in Sophy's direction. "Sophy's already had offers from a New York company, and P. J., her partner, has danced with a couple of regional companies as a soloist already."

"I'm impressed," Roxanna remarked, sounding anything but.

"Don't mind Roxy here," Carlos broke in and,

with a brotherly gesture, tousled Roxanna's carefully coiffed hair. Roxanna cringed; Sophy looked on, curious. "She's got a bone to pick with the whole ballet world these days—sort of like you with ballroom!"

"That's not true," said Roxanna, pulling away and making a big thing of rearranging her hair.

"Could have fooled me," Carlos said, not sounding very interested, but he paused to wink at Sophy.

Sophy turned away, confused. What kind of game was this guy playing? But before she could give it a second thought, she realized Laverne was talking.

"Okay, guys, listen up. I've got a real brainstorm!" the black girl announced.

Sophy and all the Academy kids moaned in unison.

"What's with you guys?" Inez asked.

"Sorry, but you don't know Laverne like we do," Shanti said. "She's definitely a flake!"

"But a creative flake!" Laverne defended herself cheerfully. "I know exactly how to make this whole thing work—that is, if you guys will let me take charge."

Roxanna jumped to her feet. "Why should we?"

"Because," Sophy hurried to Laverne's defense, "she really is gifted in the choreography department. Her dad's taught her a few things—"

"More like it's in her genes!" Daly corrected.

"And don't worry, Roxanna," Laverne assured her warmly. "I just want to take charge of the dancing—someone from Rainbow Dance can help with the rest."

"Carlos!" a couple of people yelled.

Carlos threw his hands up in protest. "Nope. Not me. Roxanna's better at organizing. I'd rather just do the dancing part."

Sophy wondered. Was Carlos just playing the nice guy? Was he just sticking up for his partner, or was he serious? Was he only into his dancing? Now *that* was something she could understand.

"So what is your plan, Laverne?" Inez asked.

"Wait. I want it to brew awhile, but we haven't got much time. Rehearsals should begin tomorrow night at the Academy, after classes." She turned toward Roxanna and Carlos. "Will that work for you guys?"

They agreed on a time, and then Laverne called for quiet. "I think you'll love my idea. And I'll make sure everyone gets to perform one way or another. But this will only work if the top dancers from each school agree to perform." Laverne looked directly at Sophy.

Sophy inhaled deeply. She noticed Roxanna put her arm protectively around Carlos. Obviously Rainbow Dance's top couple was ready to hog the show. Roxanna smiled over at Sophy. Sophy gave her a cool smile right back. She knew a challenge when she saw one.

"Count me in!" Sophy said, and a second later was smothered in hugs.

♡ ♡ ♡

"Sophy, tell her," Ray said that night in Footsteps, the dance wear store in the mall. "Tell Daly she's not getting fat."

Sophy just looked at her friend and laughed. She felt better than she had in days. She had a feeling when she told her mother about the meeting at Under Wraps her mom would be really proud of her.

Sophy liked the person she had been this afternoon. Strong, in charge, and making the best of a situation she had to live with and couldn't change.

"Daly, you are not getting fat. Ray says so. He should know. He was able to lift you in partnering class with only a couple of grunts!" Sophy squeezed in next to Daly in front of the mirror and held up a filmy blue short practice dance skirt. "Blue or red?"

"Gray," Daly pronounced. "Matches your eyes. And red makes even you look twice your size. Blue is not your color. It's mine. There's only one left on sale, but"—she checked the tag—"it's an extra small, and I'm closer to medium these days!"

Sophy considered her friend carefully. "That's crazy." She pulled a medium skirt from the rack and reached around Daly and held it up to her friend's waist. "Look. You'd drown in this."

Daly blinked at her reflection. "Can it be I look fatter than I am?"

"All that fat is in your head these days!" Ray said, sounding more than a little peeved. He started over to look at some new ballet shoes.

"Catelano! What's up?"

At the sound of Carlos's voice, Sophy caught her breath. "What's he doing here?" she murmured, half hiding behind the circular rack of skirts and practice tutus.

Daly shrugged. "Same thing we are. Shopping for shoes, I guess. What do guys wear, anyway, when they dance ballroom?"

Sophy had no idea.

"Hey, girls, look who's here," Ray announced, poking his head around the rack. Carlos, a good head taller than Ray and a little broader in the shoulders, was right behind him. He flashed a quick, nervous grin.

Daly grabbed a skirt and vanished into a dressing room. Ray went back to the shoe display. Sophy was tempted to dive beneath the clothing rack just to avoid being with Carlos.

"Funny we've never run into each other here before," Carlos remarked after a moment's silence.

"Definitely weird." Sophy was at a loss for words. Her few conversations with Carlos had been so public and charged, she felt self-conscious. Small talk seemed beside the point.

The silence stretched until Sophy thought she'd die from embarrassment. Then Daly marched up. "This outfit looks ridiculous. What was I thinking?" She shoved the hanger with the skirt back onto the rack. "We're heading over to the Sound Waves to check out that new CD by Caramel. It's supposed to have come in." Before Sophy could protest, Daly had hauled Ray out of the shop. "Back in a sec!" she called breezily over her shoulder.

Left alone with Carlos, Sophy wasn't sure what to do. She had stocked up on dance gear in New York and had only come into Footsteps to help Daly find stuff on sale.

"I've got to try on shoes," Carlos said, flagging down the salesman. He told him his size and sat down on a chair while the guy went into the store-room.

Sophy stood awkwardly, fingering some shrink-wrapped packages of tights.

Suddenly he broke the silence. "Looks like things are going to work out for us—the schools, I mean," he added quickly.

"Yeah. I guess," Sophy said, shifting from foot to foot. She looked out the shop window, into the mall atrium. Sound Waves was across the way. But Ray and Daly were in an alcove by the entrance making out. Sophy sighed. She couldn't exactly leave Footsteps to join them. Not now.

"The salesguy is taking forever," Carlos spoke again. "What I meant to say before is I'm glad you came onboard with the gala and all. It'll mean a lot to the Academy kids if you're part of things."

"Didn't have much choice, did I?" Sophy said, turning around and looking down at him. "But I guess it'll work out somehow."

He's as uncomfortable as I am, she realized. She

sat primly on the edge of the chair next to his. She had changed after dinner from her dressy linen pants to a pair of overalls and a thin-strappy undershirt and was wearing mismatched high-tops. Carlos on the other hand looked a little dressed up. He must have noticed her checking him out.

"Don't worry, these are dance duds, not the sort of stuff I wear to school—or in public much!" he laughed, fingering the neat crease in his Dockers.

Sophy relaxed slightly. "School? You're still in school?"

"Lincoln High."

"Me too," she said, turning to face him. "How come I've never seen you around before?"

"Big school—and"—he made a circle of his thumb and forefinger and studied her as if through the lense of a camera—"I bet you're not a senior."

"No such luck." Sophy sighed. She leaned back on her hands. "Just a junior. What I would give if this were my last year . . . though I'll get you mad if I tell you why," she said with a laugh. Suddenly she realized they were having something close to a normal conversation.

He put his hands up as if to ward off a blow. "Let me guess. It has to do with Rainbow Dance and the Academy merging. . . ."

She chuckled. "Sort of. I just want school to be over with so I can go off and begin my life and really dance. I had an offer from a company in New York, but—but my mother . . . " Sophy stopped herself. She barely knew this guy and she was confiding about her mother. Somehow that felt a little like betraying her mom.

"Tell me about it!" Carlos's response took her off guard.

"Your mother, too?" Sophy suddenly looked at him with new eyes. "Of course. I bet your parents aren't too hot on your dancing. Or am I wrong?" She realized she knew nothing about Carlos Vargas or his home life.

"You mean because I'm a guy?" He laughed. "It's not that bad. I know Ray's family had a hard time dealing with him and ballet. He clued me in on that this summer. No, my family, they love dancing. Men, Latino men, dance. It's generally considered pretty manly. Though if I went out for ballet, rather than social dancing, they might feel differently. No—it's just that I hate waiting around for my life to start." He broke off as the salesman finally brought him the pair of soft-soled shoes Sophy noticed that they laced up and looked pretty much like men's dress shoes.

Sophy knew what he meant about waiting for something real. While Carlos tried out the shoes, she watched him test a couple of steps, and she couldn't help but wonder if he was showing off a little for her. The idea made her feel like little feathers were tickling her insides.

He handed the salesman some money and tugged his boots back on. "Yeah, I hate putting my life on hold," he continued as if the conversation hadn't stopped. "If it were up to me I'd quit school now and just dance."

"Why don't you?" Sophy asked. "Inez says you and Roxanna are professionals—practically."

"We are," he said with a proud toss of his head. "But my parents would kill me if I quit school. And I still need to study dancing, too. Nadia Ivanov's a top teacher and coach. Besides, my scholarship at the school would be cut off if I quit high school before graduation. It's some kind of condition they put on it."

"That stinks," Sophy blurted, touching his arm.

At her touch he looked up from putting away his wallet. She dropped her hand, but held his glance. His eyes were dark, unreadable, but bright somehow, too. He seemed to see right through her, all the way to the bottom of her soul. Sophy suddenly felt frightened and very private. Her cheeks flushed, and she looked away.

Just then the door to the shop flew open.

"Carlos Vargas!" Roxanna's throaty laugh broke the spell. "I ran into Daly and Ray in Sound Waves. We had to fight over the last Caramel album. You know—the one we danced to at Leslie's party the other night." She hooked one arm through Carlos's and seemed to notice Sophy for the first time.

"Cute outfit!" she remarked, looking Sophy slowly up and down.

Roxanna was dressed in tight leather pants, an oversized silky blouse with a big metal belt cinched around her narrow waist.

Compared to Roxanna, Sophy felt like a regular mall rat.

"Nice to see you, too," Sophy countered with exaggerated sweetness. But Roxanna was already out the door with Carlos in tow, her high platform heels tapping musically against the stone floor.

Chapter Seven

The first time Inez stepped into Studio A on the second floor of the Ballet Academy, she felt as if she were stepping into church.

Except the place was bright with lights. Mirrors lined the walls, making the huge room seem twice its size. In a corner a costume rack was jam-packed with tutus. Spirits were high, and the studio buzzed with a nervous energy. Kids from Rainbow Dance were trying out the floor, posing in front of the mirrors or hanging out over by the sound equipment. Academy students warmed up at the barre. They were dressed in a hodgepodge of practice stuff. Dance pants, leggings, sweats. Not at all the way she'd seen pictures of Academy students in the school's brochure: the girls in black leotards and pink tights; the boys in white T-shirts and black tights.

Inez stopped just inside the doorway and singled out Sophy. She was wearing purple dance pants, and a T-shirt with a DANCE NEW YORK logo. Her tiny waist was cinched with a piece of black elastic. She looked casual, but unlike the other dancers at the barre, very neat and contained. Carlos was right, Inez thought. She's the real thing. Sophy's face was quiet with concentration. She looked like the calm center of a chaotic cheerful storm as she pliéd effortlessly.

Someday, Inez vowed, *I'll be just like that.*

But not now. Not yet. Inez spotted Carlos. He and Nick Oates, her new partner, were huddled over the tape deck, fine-tuning the bass on a fast, club-style salsa number. Two guys were moving a piano from one side of the room to the other. Laverne seemed to have cloned herself. She was everywhere at once. Talking to the piano movers. Consulting with Roxanna. Yelling instructions to Carlos.

"Aren't you going to warm up?" P. J. called to Inez as she crossed in front of the barre on her way to Carlos. She had brought him some tango tapes, like he'd asked.

Inez smiled shyly at P. J. He was handsome in a blond, sun-streaked way that reminded her of Brad Pitt. "No," she said softly. "I don't usually. Not for ballroom practice." But she hesitated. "I do love barre work, though," she said, then wanted to die for admitting it.

"Come on, then," Sophy said. "Kick off your shoes and work in your socks. I do it all the time at home. I don't understand how you people manage without a good warm-up."

Inez looked down at her leggings and her soft, oversized T-shirt and shrugged. "Why not?"

She sat down on the floor, pulled off her shoes, and deposited them with her backpack by the rosin box. When she stood up she wasn't sure where to place herself at the barre. Ray was there, and Daly, and Shanti and some other kids she hadn't seen before.

"Here, behind me," Sophy said, making room for her. "Have you had some ballet?" she asked, smiling at Inez in the mirror.

"Ummm—some," Inez admitted. Then wondered what music Sophy was dancing to.

Before she could ask, Sophy explained, "We're just working to counts. Like, 'down, two, three, four. Up, two, three, four.' Slow, for grande pliés. Just follow," she encouraged.

Nervously, Inez followed Sophy's count, but in her head she could hear every word of Mikhail's instructions. She turned out her legs from the hips and, keeping her knees well over her toes, sank slowly into the deep-knee bend, then with great control, slowly came up again. Her muscles trembled from the strain of moving at such a slow pace. Watching Sophy, she noticed things Sophy did differently and tried to match her style to the more experienced ballet dancer.

Then the small group began a series of petit battements and rond de jambes. Exercises Inez did faithfully every day at Rainbow Dance, whether Mikhail could help her or not. After a few grande battements, Sophy stopped.

"Wow, you really *have* studied! I'm impressed," she told Inez as she grabbed her towel from the barre and mopped the sweat off the back of her neck.

"Who's your teacher?" P. J. inquired.

"Mikhail."

"What school?" Shanti asked, sitting down to retie the ribbons on her pointe shoes.

Inez hesitated. "Rainbow Dance," she said finally.

"They have a ballet program?" Sophy exclaimed, putting on a sweatshirt.

Inez shook her head. "No. Mikhail taught me on the sly. I guess you don't remember me, but I had three or four months of dance classes here, when the school was still out at the mall."

Sophy and Daly exchanged a glance. "You used to come with your brother," they said, their voices full of wonder. "*That* scrawny guy was Carlos?" Daly shrieked, then clapped a hand over her mouth.

Inez giggled softly. "Yeah. One and the same. Anyway, I've been at Rainbow Dance for ages now. When Mikhail found out I was giving myself a barre, he stopped me. He told me to dance right or quit right then and there. So he became my teacher—I guess."

"But who is this Mikhail?" P. J. asked. "I'd sure like to know, because from the looks of you, he's a pretty good teacher."

Inez didn't know how to take the compliment. She wanted to feel proud. Still, maybe P. J. was just a nice guy. Being polite. He was waiting for her answer. "My teacher—oh, it's Mikhail Ivanov."

Sophy gaped. "Roxanna's—?"

"Father," Inez finished for her. "He was a soloist when he was young at the Kirov, when Leningrad was still Saint Petersburg. Before they moved here."

"How come we don't know about him?" Sophy wondered aloud. "High Falls's dance community is pretty small. I'm sure the MacGregors would have wanted him on staff here, even before the merger."

"He doesn't dance anymore. He can't. He had some kind of accident. No one ever talks about it." Inez suddenly felt she had said more than she should. Not that she knew much more about Roxanna's father, except that he was a very kind teacher.

"So he doesn't dance ballroom, either?" Ray asked.

"Never has, as far as I know," Inez said.

"Whatever," Sophy said, putting her hand on Inez's shoulder. "He's been a good teacher, and you sure have the makings of a real ballet dancer, Inez Vargas."

For the space of a heartbeat Inez was purely, perfectly happy.

"Nice of you to say," Roxanna remarked, coming up to the barre. She was wearing an old pair of scuffed gold ballroom heels. She arched her foot prettily and checked it in the mirror. "Inez has these illusions of becoming, well—just like you, Sophy. As if a few measly lessons could do the trick at her age."

Inez's happy bubble burst. Silently, she cursed Roxanna.

Sophy, however, leaped to Inez's defense. "From what I've seen tonight, Inez is as good as anyone in the advanced intermediate classes here. If she wants to dance ballet, her chances are as good as anyone's, Roxanna. Believe me. I saw worse at Summerdance in New York. And those girls had studied half their lives already."

Roxanna shrugged. "Whatever you say, Sophy. After all, you *are* the prima ballerina around here."

As she walked off, Inez turned to Sophy. "You're putting me on, right?"

"Wrong," Sophy said quickly.

"You'd need to work hard," P. J. chimed in, "but, hey, there's going to be *lots* of chances for that once the schools merge, right?"

Inez wanted to believe P. J. but wasn't sure. Mrs. Ivanov had her own plans for Inez. Especially since she'd found her a good partner just this week. Still, Inez could dream.

"Okay let's get to work!" Laverne shouted.

Conversations died to murmurs. Someone turned off the tape deck. The piano movers had disappeared some time ago, but Inez hadn't noticed when.

A loose semicircle formed around Laverne, kids jostling for position next to buddies and friends. Inez dropped down between Sophy and Daly.

"So what's on your mind, Laverne?" Carlos asked.

"First of all, I cleared everything already with the powers that be here. The MacGregors okayed my plans—if you all decide to go along with them."

"Generous of them," someone snickered, "but what about the Ivanovs?"

"They don't care. That's what I heard, at any rate." Laverne shrugged the comment off. She checked her clipboard. "So, first things first—sort of. Like I have permission to contact the local cable stations to try to get press coverage of our fund-raiser. I need a couple of volunteers to tackle the media, and I know just the people for the job." She eyeballed Ray and Daly. "You two would be perfect."

"Hey, that's not fair," Roxanna broke in. "Someone from Rainbow Dance should be part of any team working the publicity."

"True," Laverne admitted readily. "So, then, I can add you to the list?" she asked Roxanna.

"*Moi?* No way. I'm too busy right now. Besides, whatever we end up needing to do for this gig, Carlos and I are scheduled for a major regional competition in two weeks. We need practice time."

"Now that's the truth!" Carlos said. "I'm worried about fitting in rehearsal time here."

"We'll do it," Roxanna stated firmly. "Somehow."

Inez poked her hand in the air. "Laverne," she called out. "Ummm—I'll represent Rainbow

Dance. I'll go with Ray and Daly. If they don't mind." She turned to her new friends.

"Mind? It'll be fun. Besides, you can fill these cable dudes in on the ballroom thing. We're both totally clueless in that department," Daly told her.

Laverne wrote down Inez's name on her list. As Laverne went on to discuss other details surrounding the production of a fund-raiser, Inez hugged her knees to her chest and beamed.

Carlos was right. If you dreamed long and hard enough, your dreams had a chance of coming true. She wasn't a ballet dancer yet. Maybe she'd never make it to the professional level. But here she'd be able to dance. And already she was beginning to feel better about herself.

Life at Rainbow Dance, outside of Carlos, had been lonely. At best, Roxanna shunned her; more often, she scorned her. But already at the Academy, Inez had the feeling she was beginning to make some real friends. Daly was so warm. Ray was so generous. And Sophy Bartlett herself had told her she had what it took to be a real dancer.

♡ ♡ ♡

"So, Laverne, what about the gala? What's the plan?" Sophy asked finally, unable to stand one more second of suspense.

She'd come to the Academy that night, insides churning. Partly because she didn't quite trust Laverne to come up with something dignified enough for the gala.

Partly because Carlos would be there. She wasn't sure how to deal with him after their meeting in Footsteps. The guy unnerved her, and she wasn't used to being unnerved. She'd liked talking to him about normal things, things they had in common, like school, and dancing—talking like friends.

But could Carlos Vargas really be just another friend? Up close, he felt too in her face, too personal.

Not that Carlos had given her more than a quick "hi" tonight. He'd been off dealing with the sound equipment with the guys while she'd warmed up at the barre. Now he was halfway around the semicircle. They weren't even quite facing each other.

"I've hatched my plot," Laverne was saying as Sophy returned her attention to the meeting. "You all are going to love it!"

Sophy braced herself. Laverne was more than flaky, in Sophy's book. She was seriously unpredictable, a little on the wild side, and in some ways not to be trusted. Sophy wished she had thought things through at the meeting before she had stood up for Laverne. Could she really hold up to the pressure of being in charge?

About Laverne's creative gifts, Sophy had no doubts. She'd probably be famous some day, directing a dance company. Making great performers and performances. Sophy could dance her way out of a brown paper bag if she had to, blindfolded. But for the life of her she couldn't choreograph even a mediocre concert piece.

"Here's the deal. At our last meeting, we talked about shaping the fund-raiser around ballroom and ballet. Using both kinds of dance to show off the strengths of both schools. I asked Roxanna for a crash course in ballroom." Laverne paused to grin at Roxanna.

Roxanna preened, and a little alarm bell went off in Sophy's head. When did those two get so tight?

"So I'm equipped to play around with some basic ballroom patterns. This is the plan. We'll open the program with a demonstration of popular ballroom dances—"

"What?" one of the Academy boys cried.

"With Roxanna performing them, of course," Ray added pointedly.

"Whoever dances, that'll sure give the wrong impression," Sophy protested, scrambling to her feet. "It's bad enough the Academy is being bailed out by a ballroom school. Now we'll look like the whole ballet program itself is being taken over, done away with."

"Sure, Sophy. Just because the program opens with a ballroom dance. What would you say if it opened with ballet?" Carlos challenged.

Sophy was silenced for a moment. *Did he have a point?* Sophy searched her heart.

"Forget it, Carlos," Roxanna spoke up. "Sophy is such a snob, she can't admit that Laverne's come up with a good idea here."

"Wrong!" Sophy finally spoke up, feeling more sure of herself. "Yes, I'd feel differently if we opened with ballet, because we've been a ballet school, and we want the audience—the world—to know we still are."

"But this won't be a ballet school, Sophy Bartlett," Roxanna sparred. "It's going to be something different, whatever it's called. It is going to be at least half ballroom. You're just afraid if Rainbow Dancers get to show their stuff, people won't be interested in your poky old ballet classes."

"That's enough, Roxanna. You've made it perfectly clear that you, and probably the rest of the kids from Rainbow Dance, can't wait to get in this building, crowd our space, take over our classrooms. Eventually we'll be a footnote in your school catalog." Sophy started for the dressing room. "I've had enough. I know I said I'd be part of this, but what's the point. . . ."

"The point is, you promised," Daly called after her. Sophy stopped in her tracks. Yes. She had promised.

She turned around reluctantly. "We need you, Sophy," Ray added. "You're the best dancer we've got."

"For sure," Laverne added quickly, sounding shaken. "Hey, Bartlett, I didn't mean to tip things in the direction of Rainbow Dance, or the Academy. In fact, I've planned demonstrations of each school's strong points, danced by the top students.

You and P. J. will close with *The Sleeping Beauty* pas de deux you've been working on."

"Oh," Sophy said, trying not to meet Carlos's eyes. She suddenly felt very embarrassed. In the past few days she'd done more yelling in public than she had in her whole life. Wishing she could rub herself out with some kind of invisible ink, she rejoined the circle in the closest spot. As luck would have it, next to Carlos.

Carlos looked at her, his expression guarded. Then he turned back to Laverne. "That's all wrong, Laverne. No way ballet should close the evening."

Sophy's chest tightened. *Here we go again.* She was getting sick of all this fighting. She was beginning to feel as if he were oil and she were water.

"Why's that?" she asked. They were close enough that she could feel his muscles tense through the light fabric of his shirt.

"Because the last number of the evening is what the audience really remembers most. The point of this whole fund-raiser is to say, 'Hey, we're something new. Something you've never seen in High Falls before. You're gonna love what we do.'"

"Good point, Carlos," Roxanna purred.

"Whatever the point is, I don't get it." Sophy held her ground.

"I do," Laverne broke in, beaming. "He's right. I was wrong. The closing part belongs to everybody."

"A production number?" Daly sounded thrilled.

"A production number?" Sophy wanted to throw up.

"No," Laverne pondered. "Just a switch in the program order. I think the end will be some ballroom-ballet combo routine." She bit her lip, checked her notes, and looked up at Sophy. "How about a tango with the girl on pointe? You and Carlos made quite a team the other night at Rainbow Dance."

"Me and Carlos?" Sophy blurted. Impossible. All those rehearsals. All that time alone. Sophy couldn't survive that. Carlos was too intense, too—suddenly she remembered the tango music. The way it had pierced her to the heart, but seemed to root her to the floor. She had had no idea how to move to it. No, this would not work.

"Me? Dancing with Sophy on pointe? Like a ballet dancer?" Carlos sounded less than enthused.

He looked at Sophy. She looked at him. *He hates this as much as I do.*

"You won't have to dance ballet steps, Carlos. You'll do your usual ballroom routine, with a few changes. It'll be fun." Laverne sat forward expectantly.

"Funny's more like it," Roxanna grumbled.

Laverne elbowed her. "Lighten up, Roxy," she teased.

Carlos didn't seem to hear her. He studied the floor, then looked up and cracked a small smile. "I'm game," he said. "What's to lose? It'll be worth seeing the expression on my parents' faces when I say I'm in a ballet."

Inez started laughing. "Papa will hate it."

"But, hey, I might learn something!"

"That puts a new spin on it," Roxanna pouted. "A learning experience. I used to dance on pointe a bit. Just a couple of years ago. Maybe I could dance with Carlos, and . . ."

"I'll do it," Sophy interrupted before Roxanna had a chance to change Laverne's mind. "I might learn something, too."

Carlos swallowed visibly and poked out his hand. "It's a deal."

Sophy shook it. His palm was sweaty like hers. *He's as nervous as I am,* Sophy realized. It was as if they were suddenly two sides of the same coin.

"Isn't that cozy?" Roxanna sneered. "I mean, like they've never really danced together. It'll be a mess, and—"

"Roxanna, quiet," Laverne ordered firmly. "I have something very special planned for you, too. How does dancing the Black Swan in heels sound? With P. J., maybe? He's always our resident prince."

"If you put it that way . . . " Roxanna gave a delighted shiver. "The Black Swan sounds luscious, and rich, and isn't she sort of sexy and bad?"

"The worst!" remarked Sophy half to herself.

"Pure evil!" said Laverne out loud.

Chapter Eight

 Tuesday after school, Daly stepped out of the front doors of Lincoln High, into the blinding afternoon light.

"Daly. Over here!" Inez shouted. Daly shielded her eyes. After a moment, she spotted Inez waving from over by the monument, just off the path leading to the parking lot.

Daly bounded down the steps and threaded her way through the knots of students. "Ray here yet?" she asked as she walked up. Ray, Inez, and Daly had made an appointment to visit the WHF-TV studios after school, to talk up the fund-raiser at the Academy.

Inez shook her head. Her hair just touched her shoulders and shone blue black in the sun.

Dumping her book bag on the ground, Daly hoisted herself up on the base of the monument and kicked her feet against the base. "He usually gets hung up in bio lab. The teacher's a real creep about performing arts students having special schedules."

"What time's our appointment at WHF-TV?" Inez asked, checking her watch.

"The woman I spoke with said anytime between four and four-thirty would be good," Daly answered, then she giggled softly. "But I'm glad Ray's not here yet. I want to ask you something about your brother—privately."

"Carlos?"

"Yeah. Has he got a girlfriend?" Daly inquired.

Inez pointed at Daly and laughed. "What you really want to know is whether he and Roxanna are an item."

"I'm that transparent." Daly sighed, fingering the hole in the knee of her jeans. "My mother always tells me I have a face like an open book."

"Maybe, maybe not," Inez said, gathering her hair up into a low ponytail and clipping it with a big orange barrette. "Everyone's curious about those two."

"Even you?" Daly probed.

"I have my suspicions—"

"Which are?"

Inez shook her head. "No. Not that Carlos wouldn't date her. He manages to fit in a lot of girls," Inez laughed. "He's not the shy type that way."

So Carlos has been around. Daly figured as much. She filed that information away, for Sophy, not for now, but for someday.

"But he's got this thing about not dating partners. And besides, I don't think she's really his type."

Daly started to ask if, maybe, Sophy by any chance was his type, but just then Ray sprinted up.

"Sorry I'm late," he said, smiling at Inez, then holding his hands up toward Daly, seated on the monument. She reached for him and jumped lightly down to the ground. He caught her by the waist and kissed her right on the mouth. For a second she kissed him back, then remembered Inez. She pulled back and just took Ray's hand.

"My car's the red-and-green Bug over at the far end of the lot," he told Inez as they all headed across the grass.

A few minutes later they had snaked out into the line of traffic leading down the long front drive to the school, out to Main. "We've still got lots of time before we head to the TV studio," Ray said. "I'm starved. Anyone else hungry?"

"I could eat a house," Inez said, patting her flat stomach. "And we're right near Baily's Burgers. They've got a mean special on fries and double burgers this week."

"Are you sure we won't be late?" Daly asked, hoping they wouldn't stop for food. She'd been perfect so far today. Eating only one slice of bread for breakfast, with a teaspoon of diet jam. She'd skipped lunch entirely. With any luck she could keep herself to under five hundred calories. But not if she stopped at the burger joint. Not with her stomach growling and her head hurting.

"Meaning," said Ray, giving her a sidewards glance, "that you don't want to be within five miles of food."

Inez did a double take. "Don't tell me you're *dieting?*"

Daly shrugged. "I've got to watch everything I eat. If I think cookie, I put on five pounds," she joked as Ray signaled, then turned into the lot of the fast-food restaurant.

Inez gave Daly a good, hard look as they headed inside. "Well, you don't look at all fat to me."

"Me either," added Ray pointedly. "But try to convince Ms. Starvation Diet of that."

"I'm not on a starvation diet. Truth is, I'm not the least bit hungry," Daly lied. Actually, Daly was positively drooling at the sight of all those double burgers and cheese fries. "I'll just have a diet soda."

Inez grabbed a table, and Ray and Daly deposited their stuff on the chairs. Ray waited until Inez was out of earshot. Just short of the counter, he turned and told Daly, "This is getting crazy. You never eat anymore."

"Stop it, Ray. I do," Daly protested. But to be sure he believed her, she left him at the cashier, stepped right up to the next register, and placed an order for large fries.

"You'll have to wait a sec," the cashier told her. "We're cooking up a fresh batch." Daly stepped aside to let the next customer step up to the counter.

"Did you hear," a woman's voice said from somewhere behind Daly, "that there's talk of yet another downsizing?" Daly looked behind her, but the women were hidden behind the wall of a booth.

"More people being laid off?" a second voice responded, astounded. "Why, it's positively sinful, all these people suddenly without work, and families to support."

"Tell me about it," the first woman exclaimed. "When the first round of managers got their pink slips, we had a mortgage to pay and two kids still in college. If I hadn't gotten that job as a clerk in admissions at the university, we would have lost the house."

"Your fries," the cashier told Daly.

"Did you hear those women talking?" Daly asked Ray as they headed back toward Inez and their table.

"About the downsizing? Yeah, scary stuff."

"Wonder what company they were talking about?" she asked Ray.

"Didn't catch the name."

Trying not to look too obvious, Daly turned around to see if the women were still in the booth across the way. She carefully let a fry fall as she passed. "Whoops!" she muttered, and stooped to pick it up. She took a quick look at the table, and her heart stopped. It was Mrs. Mullane, and her friend who taught home ec in the middle school.

Mrs. Mullane's husband had worked at High Falls Fabricators, the plant that assembled lawn furniture out near I-80. The plant where Daly's father worked.

"Daly?" Ray had come back to find her.

"Oh, I dropped this," she said, scrambling to her feet. She brandished the fry and tossed it in the garbage. But as she followed Ray back to their table, her knees felt like Jell-O. She didn't know much about downsizing. But her parents had seemed worried lately. All those midnight gab sessions in the kitchen. Was her dad about to lose his job?

♡ ♡ ♡

Roxanna slammed the door to her room and covered her ears with her hands. "Just shut up!" she begged, but softly, so no one could hear her. Whenever her parents fought like this, she tried to make herself invisible. To stay out of harm's way.

Not that fights in the Ivanov home ever got physical.

But sometimes words could hurt as much as a fist, and her mother was queen of the put-down line. "Now that's who should be dancing the Black Swan," Roxanna muttered.

She slid her back down the door and sat on the floor. She squeezed her eyes shut and hugged her knees to her chest. "Stop them, please," Roxanna prayed, not sure anymore if anyone ever listened to her prayers. Tonight's fight was going to rate fifteen on a scale of one to ten. Already they'd started hurling curses at each other in Russian. Some words Roxanna knew; others, she could only guess the meaning of. For every word her father yelled, her mother shouted ten more, ten times louder.

Not that she could really blame her mother completely. Her father was enough to drive any woman crazy. Ever since that dumb accident, he'd been impossible. He refused to have anything to do with dance. His name was on the school because her mother insisted. But what was the point? All he did was drive a cab. And when he was off duty at the garage, then he took to drink. When he drank, her mother laid into him.

What was that line? *It takes two to tango.*

Cute phrase, especially given what went down yesterday at the Academy. That conniving little Sophy Bartlett had wormed her way into dancing with Carlos after all. The thought of Carlos even touching Sophy, even in the make-believe world of the dance, drove Roxanna crazy. But then the whole idea was crazy. Sophy was so cold. Carlos so hot. The two of them couldn't even salsa well together. That was perfectly obvious the other night. Laverne was out of her mind pairing them up.

Maybe Sophy had bribed Laverne. Maybe Laverne and Sophy were good friends....

Roxanna tried to picture that. Nah! Sophy was so uptight. A real play-by-the-rules sort of girl. Laverne seemed anything but. She was a soul mate if Roxanna had ever met one. Someone who liked to live a little on the edge, test her limits, meet the guys who weren't Mr. All-American Apple Pie. Guys like Carlos. One thing was for sure: Sophy didn't know what she was getting herself into with Carlos.

Carlos was playing his own game, one that

Roxanna didn't understand yet, but she'd figure him out soon. He was all passion with a big dream. And if Roxanna's suspicions were right, a little ballerina never could be part of it.

Meanwhile there were other fish in the sea. If Carlos thought he was making her jealous, Roxanna would give him a taste of his own medicine. She thought a minute, then a slow smile crept across her face. She knew exactly where to meet some hot guys. Guys who appreciated really good dancers. Roxanna reached for her phone and dialed a number scrawled in the back of her loose-leaf book.

Laverne picked up on the second ring.

"Hi, it's me, Roxanna!"

"Oh, hi!" Laverne sounded happy.

Roxanna flopped down on her bed and stared at the ceiling. "Whatcha up to tonight?"

Laverne chuckled. "Nothing—though I'm supposed to be buried in books. We've got some lit paper due soon. How about you?"

"I was thinking of doing a little research. . . ."

"Research!" Laverne made a barfy sort of noise.

"Hear me out," Roxanna said smoothly. "If you're going to choreograph all this ballroom dance material, you should take a field trip."

"I've been to Rainbow Dance. You know that."

Roxanna didn't quite remember ever seeing Laverne there, but the place was big and usually crowded. "But that's not the real thing, you know. Have you ever been to one of the off-campus dance clubs down by the waterfront?"

"You mean like Milongas, or Tangos and Sauce?" Laverne sounded shocked. "Of course not. I'm underage. Who'd let me in?"

"You could pass for twenty-one, with a bit more makeup. Are you game?"

Laverne was silent. Then she laughed a low laugh. "I'm always game, for something."

"Figured that," Roxanna practically cheered. "I'll scare up some ID. Dress hot, with heels, and wear lots of makeup. Oh"—Roxanna had almost forgotten—"will you have trouble getting out of the house?"

"Are you kidding?" Laverne scoffed. "Dad's away on business this week, and Mrs. B., our house-keeper, sleeps like a log. Believe me, I could practically throw a party here and she wouldn't notice."

"Great," Roxanna remarked. "See you, then, in say a half hour on the corner of Green near Tangos and Sauce." Roxanna hung up, hugged herself, and smiled so hard, her face hurt.

Tonight she was out for some real fun. For once she'd found a partner in crime and she loved it. Besides, becoming friends with Laverne might have some fringe benefits. She might even con her into offering Roxanna another plum part, something she could dance with Carlos. Something sultry and showy. Something to bring the house down. She savored the picture until the clock chimed in the hall, breaking her daydream.

She flung open her closet and plunged into a sea of short, clingy dresses and leather skirts. She fingered through her tops, seeking just the right one. Tonight she wanted to look just perfect.

♡　♡　♡

Hyped and ready to party, Laverne Grey stood outside of Tangos and Sauce, wondering if bouncers could smell fear. She had read somewhere that watchdogs could. But this wasn't fear. Terror was more like it. Her adrenaline was flowing. Her pulse was racing. And she was pumped.

She was also convinced Roxanna was about to make fools of them both. "This is *not* going to work," she told the Russian girl in an undertone. "We don't even have IDs. Besides, I'm sure I don't look even eighteen, let alone twenty-one."

"Believe me, in that outfit and with that hair, you look at least twenty-one."

Laverne tugged down her blue metallic stretch skirt and hoped Roxanna was right. Inspired by her favorite NBA jock, she had sprayed a streak of bright blue in her black short-cropped hair.

"Let me do the talking!" Roxanna instructed under her breath.

Laverne buttoned her lips, her eyes darting up and down the line straggling toward the entrance to the club. Half the kids were really dressed to dance; the other half wore jeans. Smokers were clustered off to the side, laughing loudly, sounding a little self-conscious. But everyone looked a lot older than sixteen. *Not bad,* she thought, checking out some guys on the line. Roxanna had been right: High school boys were the pits; these guys were more like real men.

The line inched forward, and then they were at the makeshift ticket window. Roxanna smiled demurely at the guy behind the desk. He was Latino, and looked a little like Carlos, but taller, bigger—older. "Two, please," Roxanna purred, pushing a twenty-dollar bill toward the cash box.

Without a second glance the guy stamped both their hands. A moment later Laverne found herself drowning in an ocean of noise and a sea of bodies. Her first impulse was to run right back out the door. "This place is nuts!" she said, reaching for Roxanna's arm. Laverne was afraid she'd lose her new friend in the crowd. The club looked like some scene from a steamy movie. Except for the lack of smoke. But smoking seemed to be the only thing people *weren't* doing. Couples were necking in corners, frat boys were drinking, half the place was gyrating and swirling to a heavy salsa beat. It looked like good college fun. Except Laverne felt distinctly in over her head, out of her element. Maybe she should have listened to herself and just stayed home.

"For a Tuesday night," Roxanna shouted over the din of the music, "this place is bursting at the seams. Guess it's because The Salsa Connection is scheduled to play the second set tonight."

"They're really hot," Laverne remarked, glad again she'd come.

"Same goes for you, Little Ms. Blue," a male voice remarked.

Laverne turned just as the owner of the voice began to tap her on the shoulder. For a minute she thought she was about to be carded. "Want to dance?" the guy asked.

He was tall, lanky, with coffee-colored skin and a nice-enough smile. "Why not?" Laverne shrugged, and caught Roxanna's eye. Roxanna nodded approval, then a moment later vanished in the crowd. The guy took Laverne's hand and helped her through the maze of tables, waiters, and kids hanging out.

The crowd thinned by about a millimeter toward the center of the room. When the guy put one arm around her waist and began moving in time to the merengue tune the band was playing, Laverne figured they had found the dance floor. For a moment Laverne felt uncomfortable dancing with this person with no name, in such close quarters, to such a sexy tune. But soon the dancer in her took over, and she let herself go, swaying her hips in time with the music, smiling and laughing with the guy as if they were having the funniest conversation.

The music stopped; the guy applauded her. "You're one hot dancer—by the way, I'm Willie. Willie Lopez. You go to school at High Falls U?"

Laverne nodded. She couldn't remember what

year she'd be in if she were really twenty-one. "I'm a dance major," she told him, suddenly inspired.

"Wow. Surprised I haven't seen you around before. I'm in Corley's improv class."

"An actor," Laverne beamed. She had always adored actors.

Willie gave her a funny look. "You're putting me on—right?"

For a split second Laverne hesitated. Did he mean an improv dance class? Well, she could wing it. "You bet I am. It's the heat in here. Fries the brain cells."

"I've got a cure for that," Willie said, putting an arm around her shoulder and guiding her to the bar. "Two drafts, please," he ordered.

"Beer?" Laverne squeaked.

"Something else?" Willie asked, stopping the bartender before he poured the second stein.

Now what? Laverne looked around for Roxanna. The last thing she felt like was trying a beer. Her first beer. Her father was a real teetotaler. He was against all liquor and didn't even have wine in the house. Now she was about to have her first drink. Here, with a strange guy in a club packed with strangers. But . . . she looked up at Willie; his eyes were studying her. She couldn't let him suspect that she wasn't even eighteen. He'd drop her fast, and she wasn't ready to risk that. Dancing with him had felt good. Talking wasn't bad, either.

"No. Beer's good. A draft's good," she said, hoping

she had the lingo down. He handed her one of the steins. She took her first sip and struggled not to make a face.

"That goes down nice!" Willie said, surveying the dance floor. "Let's drink up and catch a dance or two before the big men come on to play live."

Laverne held her breath and took a second gulp of beer. This time it went down easier and felt cold and good in her throat. Before she knew it, she had reached the bottom of the mug, and suddenly the room was spinning. She started to lose her balance. Willie grabbed her.

"You okay?" he asked, putting his arm around her waist and holding her up.

"Fine. I'm fine," Laverne said, finding it hard to get the words out. She felt all blurred or slurred. Was she actually drunk after just one beer?

The salsa music started, and Willie pulled her back to the dance floor. "Do you break on two?" he shouted over the music.

"What?" she shouted back. She had never danced salsa in her whole life. At Rainbow Dance she had turned up only for swing evenings.

"Never mind. Just follow me and dance."

Three measures into the music, Laverne had caught the hang of it. Willie had a tight, funky style, and Laverne mimicked him perfectly. Maybe it was the beer, but she felt loose and lanky, and as if her hips were made to swivel. Soon a crowd gathered around them, clapping in time to the music, shouting at them, cheering. Willie grabbed Laverne and spun her in a wild series of turns. Her stomach lurched, but she ignored her insides. She was having the time of her life.

The music ended, and she fell breathless and dizzy into Willie's arms. He nuzzled her head. "You're magic. You're pure magic!" he told her.

She felt his lips brush her cheeks. *No,* she thought. I don't know this guy at all yet. She liked him, but not all that much, not yet. "Willie," she said, pushing herself away a bit. "Let's dance some more. Okay?"

But before he could answer, another guy cut in. He was wearing a Beta Phi sweatshirt with the sleeves cut off, baring his bulging biceps. "My dance this time." His voice was husky, his blue eyes bloodshot red. He teetered as he reached for Laverne.

She backed up against Willie. "Um, I've already got a partner." Her voice came out squeaky and small, and her tongue felt a little thick. The beer. The dumb beer, she realized.

Mr. Muscles didn't seem to hear a word she said. He clasped her narrow wrist and began pulling her onto the dance floor.

"The lady said she's already got a partner," Willie exclaimed.

"So, what's it to you?" the frat guy bristled.

"I'm the partner."

Laverne looked from Willie to the other guy. "Look, I'm really not in the mood for dancing," she said, backing off a little. Things were getting scary here.

"Did ya hear that?" The frat guy was nose to nose with Willie. "The little lady doesn't want to dance anymore. So get lost."

"I'm not getting lost," Willie said, standing his ground.

Then the big guy hauled back and threw a punch. It went wide, grazing Willie's cheek. Laverne screamed, "Stop this!" Then a hand yanked her backward into the heart of the crowd.

"Fight, fight!" excited voices took up the cry.

Suddenly bodies were pressing forward. Chairs began to fly. But Laverne found herself pulled out of the melee. It took a minute before she finally was able to turn around. She found herself outside the kitchen, with Roxanna. "You rescued me," she gasped, feeling as if her head were on spin cycle. "I owe you one."

Roxanna nodded, but suddenly looked very young and extremely scared. "Let's get out of here before they call the cops. When they figure out high school kids were in the middle of all of this, we're going to get into major league trouble."

Laverne didn't need prompting. She followed Roxanna through the kitchen and out the door. They were safely down the block by the time the cop cars showed up. Roxanna pulled Laverne back into the bushes. The girls sat huddled together, perfectly silent for what felt like forever. As soon as the police went into the club, Roxanna darted out of the foliage and around the corner.

Laverne ran after her, cursing her high heels with every step. Finally she stopped and ripped them off. Then she ran barefoot, catching up with Roxanna at the bus stop. "That was close," Roxanna said as Laverne held her side and gasped for air.

"Are we going to get in trouble?" Laverne asked as soon as she could talk.

"How? No one knows who we are."

Laverne caught her breath. Had she told Willie her name? She couldn't remember. She didn't think so. "But I don't think it's so smart, Roxy, to hang out here waiting for the bus."

"They're still running," Roxanna said, sitting down heavily on the bench inside the Plexiglas shelter.

"Yeah, but if the cops come by and see us dressed like this . . . besides," Laverne added, looking around "it's deserted. I don't feel safe here." They had run clear past the campus and were standing just west of the university. The riverfront was only a block away.

"Why worry? Nothing ever happens in this town," Roxanna said.

"I don't care. I'm calling a cab." Laverne dug in her purse for a quarter.

"Don't," Roxanna said, jumping up. She put a hand on Laverne's arm. "Don't do that." Her voice sounded shrill.

"Like, what's the big deal—" Laverne bit her lip. Money wasn't an issue in her family, but she didn't know about the Ivanovs. Sure they could do some business deal with the Academy, but maybe they were secretly poor. "I'll spring for it. I'm flush this week," Laverne said.

"It's not—" Roxanna started, then cut herself off.

"Look, I'm not going to argue," Laverne said. She walked to the corner and popped her coins in the pay phone. She ordered a cab, gave her location, and went back to the bus stop. "They'll be here in less than five . . . Roxanna?" Laverne looked around. Roxanna had vanished.

"That girl is crazy. I hope she doesn't try to walk home." Laverne had barely started to worry when the cab pulled up. She climbed in and gave the driver her address.

"That is near ballet school, no?" he asked in a heavy accent. "Across street?"

Laverne just grunted. Her head was beginning to pound, and her stomach was about to turn inside out. That beer—yuck! Well, she wouldn't do that again.

"You ballet teacher there?"

"Me? A teacher?" Laverne started to laugh, but it hurt too much. "No," she said, massaging her temples. "I'm a student."

"Oh. You are out late, then, for a student."

"Believe me, later than I want to be," Laverne said, trying to place his accent. It had a familiar cadence. If she hadn't felt so sick, she'd have asked him where he was from. She almost started to, but her mouth felt woolly. Then he pulled up to the curb outside the two-family house where she lived with her dad. She paid the guy, then headed up the steps to the porch. She fumbled in her bag for the key.

Only when she got inside did the cab pull away. "Nice guy," she said, feeling grateful. She'd had enough scares tonight. It was good when a cab driver waited until you were safely home before driving away.

Chapter Nine

"Has Laverne lost it, or what?" Carlos complained loudly the next morning. He stopped pacing the length of the small ballet studio just long enough to stare at Sophy in the mirror.

"Don't yell at me," Sophy told him irritably. "As my sister's fond of telling me I'm not a morning person. Leaving the house before seven A.M. should be outlawed. It wasn't *my* idea to have our first practice before sunrise."

"Sunrise was over an hour ago," Carlos pointed out archly. At least he wasn't shouting. Shouting in the morning was something Sophy hated. One shouting session before breakfast a week was all she could tolerate.

"Well, we've been here almost that long. Whatever possessed Laverne to schedule this so early?"

Carlos paced over to the front window. He flung it open. A mild breeze blew in as he leaned out looking for Laverne. He ducked back in. "She's nowhere in sight. And she scheduled the rehearsal early because we have a lot of practice to fit in. The fund-raiser's at the end of next week. That doesn't leave much time to get it in shape."

"True," Sophy conceded. "But what good does it all do if she doesn't turn up? We haven't got anything to practice."

Carlos sort of shrugged and paced back toward Sophy. " Does she live far?"

"No," Sophy said. "A block from here."

"Maybe she forgot. Maybe we should call."

"We can't. House rules—Grey house rules, that is. Her dad travels a lot. Works late mounting shows. Takes the red-eye back and forth from the Coast. No calls before 10 A.M. Unless there's a big emergency." Sophy paused. "Is this an emergency?"

Carlos let out a laugh and leaned back with his elbows propped on the barre. He was dressed in jeans and a short-sleeved dark red T-shirt with the sleeves rolled up. He studied his long legs. "No. It's not an emergency, though we'll both have to leave for school in half an hour." He straightened up and executed a jazzy turn in front of the mirror. "All this hanging around, wasting time, drives me crazy."

"Me too, but what can we do? Until Laverne tells us what to dance, we can't practice."

"Maybe not," Carlos said, stroking his chin. "Sophy, remember the other night, when we tangoed?"

How could she forget? "Yeah."

"You'd never done it before."

"I'd never *seen* it before," she admitted.

"So now's the chance. I have a few clips on tape I put together for Laverne. I cued them in the VCR before you got here this morning. Let's check them out. Afterward, if she still hasn't shown, I'll start teaching you the right way to tango."

Sophy showed Carlos where the exercise mats were stashed. They pulled two out and sat down in front of the small studio monitor. He turned on the tape. "This is only a couple of minutes' footage—"

For a second Sophy didn't recognize the sophisticated couple. The tux, the incredibly form-fitting longish black dress . . . "It's you. It's you and Roxanna!" she gasped. Their steamy performance on the screen was so sophisticated, so smooth, so sexy. Sophy's cheeks began to get hot. But, still— "You look so professional. So polished!" Then she felt stupid saying that.

"It's the only stuff I could lay my hands on that showed what we call American tango now." Carlos sounded pleased and proud. "Check out the style a moment. Then watch this." He fast-forwarded to another clip.

The people on screen weren't teenagers. The male dancer was older than most kids' fathers who Sophy knew. He was even a little fat. But she forgot all of that as he gathered a curvy red-headed woman in his arms. "It looks like a tango, but—" Sophy couldn't quite explain the difference. She was mesmerized by the dark passion of the music, the intricacy of the steps, and the way the couple stared into each other's eyes.

"That's Argentinean tango," Carlos explained.

moving as one 139

"It's really hot now. And this stuff is from that PBS special last month, *Tango Salon*." Then he explained how all tangos originated in Argentina; at first, just in waterfront bars. "The dance became respectable in the twenties, and everyone began dancing it in salons. It moved to Paris. Spain. America. Then back to Argentina. But all along people had never stopped dancing it in Buenos Aires. And a new style had developed. There's more, but you can read about it some time. Nadia gave us notes to study." The tape stopped, and Carlos stood up and held out his hand to Sophy.

"Laverne is definitely still missing. Shall we start?"

Sophy stood up. What had she gotten herself into? She tried to copy the position of the woman's hands and arms.

"No, not tango hold. Not yet," Carlos said, suddenly sounding all business. Then he gave her what he called a tango barre. He didn't use music. He just counted beats. More knee bends. Easy, except he made her stand with her feet pointed straight ahead, not turned out. Then he said, "Tango is really about a walk. A kind of insolent, sultry walk." He demonstrated for her, turning back over his shoulder to say, "Hide your knees. One leg comes right in front of the other." Then he showed her other things. A sliding step to the side. Some intricate pattern where the feet swivelled. "They're called in Spanish ochos."

Sophy remembered the word from Spanish class. "That means 'eights.'" Then she laughed. "They *are* like figure eights."

"You're good at that, but then you're already a dancer," he said.

Finally he put on music and stepped up to her. "Now this," he said, taking her hands and putting them on his upper arms, "is practice position. We'll start like this."

The position left a good foot between them, which suited Sophy perfectly. "Just follow, and remember all you can about the technique. And," he added, looking down at her feet, "pretend you have heels on. Tango was built around women in heels."

Sophy had on old broken-down pointe shoes. The kind she used for practice and when she didn't need much support.

He listened to the music, letting a flowery introduction pass before he took his first step. Sophy tried to follow him. But thinking about what her feet were supposed to be doing, she stumbled and got confused. "This is hard!" she exclaimed as she tripped over her own foot. She stopped to rub her ankle.

"Of course it is," Carlos said with a trace of sarcasm. "Sooner or later I knew you'd figure that out—once you tried to dance it."

He sounded so arch, Sophy wanted to zap him with the perfect comeback.

Before she got a chance, he added, sounding

faintly apologetic, his eyes twinkling, "Though if you showed me some of those ballet steps you do, or made me dance on pointe, I'd have to admit what you do is really beyond me."

"Can't quite picture you in a tutu," Sophy admitted, returning his smile.

"But I can sure picture you in a tango dress. Hey, let's try really dancing it. I'll strut my best tango stuff. You've got your toe shoes on. . . ."

This time he held his arms out and showed her the proper tango hold. The music started, and he kept the pattern of the dance simple enough for her to follow. After a few basic box-type steps, he guided her into a series of ochos. She leaned into him a little, then stepped on pointe and tried them out that way. The sinuous movement suited her limber body, and she stayed on pointe as he repeated the whole pattern: the box, the rocking back and forth, the ochos. The music built, and died, and built again. Sophy scarcely noticed it had become one with her, one with her dancing, one with Carlos. Then it stopped. She was still on the tip of her toes. Eye to eye with Carlos.

He touched her face, and little slivers of fire coursed down her spine. "When you tango," he said in a strangely soft voice, "you look either here"—he pointed to the space between her right arm and his left—"or in your partner's eyes. Poets say the tango is a secret danced by two people."

His words hung in the air. Sophy slowly came

down off pointe, but was still holding on to him. "That's beautiful," she tried to say, but her mouth was too dry, and her heart was pounding.

His head began to lower over hers. Her lips began to part.

"Oh guys, am I late or what!" Laverne burst in.

Sophy and Carlos stepped a good three feet apart. "Um—" Sophy couldn't find her voice. Her whole body seemed to be shaking. She suddenly felt cold, then hot, then as if her feet would slip right out from under her. *Thank you, Laverne!* she said silently, and took three very deep breaths.

She looked sideward at Carlos. He seemed calm, unfazed. But he couldn't fool her. What had almost happened had really almost happened. The two little red spots burning on his cheeks gave him away. "You could have called," Carlos said sharply to Laverne. "I mean, we've wasted all this time." His voice sounded a little weird. He walked over to the window and leaned out. When he faced the room again, his color was back to normal and he walked up to Laverne.

"So. What happened?"

"I—I didn't feel well," Laverne said. For the first time Sophy really looked at her. Laverne's hair was wet from the shower. Beneath her makeup she looked sort of olive green.

Sophy hurried up to her and felt her head. Laverne flinched at her touch. "Headache—the Excedrin kind, I think."

Sophy giggled. "You look like the picture of a person with a hangover."

Carlos scoffed. "More like a girl with the flu. Why don't you go home? Skip school."

"Flu. Maybe that's it." Laverne gave Carlos a look of pure gratitude. "Mrs. B. was right. I should have stayed home. We should reschedule this practice."

"We will," Sophy said firmly. "But not now. Besides, my mom's picking me up downstairs to get me to school. I've got to leave now."

"Oh—you have a ride?" Carlos said.

"Yes." Sophy answered, but wondered what might have happened on the way to school in Carlos's truck if she didn't.

♡ ♡ ♡

"*¿Qué pasa,* Mama?" Carlos asked his mother as he tossed his books on a bench by the kitchen door.

"Not much," she answered, looking up from the stove. Her smile looked halfhearted and tired. She was still wearing shoes and stockings and a skirt. She was looking thin.

"Home late from work?" he asked, reaching for a spoon to sample the rice and beans. Someday he'd be rich enough to change all this. Someday he'd hire his mother her own cleaning woman.

"New job. A house on Vine, over by the university. It's big. Wait," She lightly batted his hand away from the pot. "It's not done yet. So I'm late and you're home early for a change from that dance place."

"Always *that* dance place," Carlos remarked. "You know the name, Rainbow Dance. Though pretty soon the name will change." He hung out a couple of minutes longer, hoping she'd ask him about the new school, about his practice with Roxanna, about the competition coming up soon. But as usual she could care less, so he headed for his room.

He felt down, and tired, and weirdly edgy all at once. "Weird" was the operative word here. The day had started out weird, with Laverne late, and him left alone all that time with Sophy.

Then tonight during their practice session, Roxanna's mother had been on the warpath. And for some mysterious reason Roxy's father, the mysterious Mikhail, kept lurking around the studio. Sometimes the guy gave Carlos the creeps, and privately he'd be just as glad when Inez could take ballet lessons in a class full of people at the Academy in a few weeks. Meanwhile whatever Carlos did on the dance floor tonight was wrong. Nothing Roxanna could do was right. Usually the girl was a dynamite dancer, but today she'd felt like she weighed about two tons in his arms, kept missing steps, and danced completely off the music. Nadia cut the session short, yelled at Roxanna, and sent Carlos home.

Now, after a shower and change of clothes, he felt better. As he combed his hair in front of the mirror, his thoughts turned back to Sophy. *Face it,*

moving as one 145

Vargas, you're hooked. No point denying the fact. Dancing with Roxanna tonight had been pure torture. Dancing with Sophy this morning had been a dream. Though there wasn't much to be done about it. Even if Sophy wanted to learn ballroom. And when it came to Sophy, his dreams weren't really about dancing.

They were from two different worlds. For all he knew her mother might be the person who lived on Vine. His mother's new employer. Carlos's mother cleaned houses to bring in extra money. Sophy's mother was a professor who probably had her house cleaned. Who knew what Sophy's father did? Carlos was pretty sure he wasn't a welder with an auto repair shop, like his dad.

"Hey, Vargas, you out of the shower or what?"

"José!" Carlos threw open his door and slapped his best friend five. Behind José, Jonny Torres was grinning. Jonny's pal from the copy shop where he worked after school was with him. "Daniel!" Carlos greeted him. "So what's up?" Carlos leaned back against the hallway wall and jammed his hands in his pockets.

"We're heading over to Milongas to hear some music. Dance a little"—José did a few steps—"hang for a while."

"Before school sets in seriously," Daniel added.

"Wanna come?" Jonny invited.

The invite zapped his blues. He rubbed his hands together gleefully. "Do you have to ask?" He ducked into his room to grab his wallet, his jacket, and the keys to his truck. "Let's hit the road. How'd you guys get here? I've got wheels."

"Great, 'cause we don't. We ran into each other at Patels's down the block, then saw the flyer about Milongas."

Carlos followed the guys out into the kitchen. As he reached for his jacket the door opened, and his father walked in.

"Carlos!" Pedro Vargas lit up at the sight of his son. His smile faded at the sight of his friends. "Where are you going on a school night?"

"Don't worry, Pop," Carlos said. "Homework's on the light side. It's just the second week of school. I won't be late." He started past his father. "We're headed for Milongas to catch the first set."

"Milongas? That club by the waterfront? Forget it. No son of mine is going to hang out there, just to get arrested."

"Arrested?" Carlos repeated, shocked. The guys shared a glance.

Jonny shrugged. "It's a nice place, Mr. Vargas. Wild kids don't run there."

Carlos's father snorted and hung his cap on the coatrack. "Just like that tango place near the campus is supposed to be a nice place. It's so nice, it was raided last night. Some brawl broke out. Two underage girls were involved, according to the news. Now that's what I call really nice."

"You guys hear about this?" Carlos asked his friends. No one had.

"Maybe it was some kind of mistake," José suggested. "Maybe the cops went to the wrong bar. Some downtown clubs are a bit rough."

"Right, wrong, I don't care," Carlos's father stated firmly. "You aren't going to Milongas. Tonight or any other night."

Carlos felt his temper rise. He saw the guys exchange a glance. "Dad," he said, forcing himself to sound calm. "Milongas isn't some kind of dive. Great jazz bands play there. Uncle Alfonso has given salsa demos there on salsa night."

"What that stupid brother of mine does is none of your business. Just because he ruined his life by dancing, you're not going to ruin yours. You're seventeen. You're almost finished school and what do you know?" Pedro Vargas shaped a big zero with his fingers. "*Nada.* Nothing. All you care about is dancing. Well, look at Alfonso. Where has all this dancing got him? You still have a chance. Next year you learn welding; you take over my business when you're older."

"Right. Vargas and Sons! Forget it, Dad."

"He's right," Carlos's mother broke in, wiping her hands on her apron. "Carlos is not made to be a welder. He is good in school. He'd be better if he worked at it instead of wasting all his time at that dance place. He should go to college, not settle for this sort of life. He can do better, Pedro."

"Nothing's wrong with what I do. How we live . . . "

Carlos gestured with his head. Jonny opened the door softly. While his parents argued, Carlos followed his friends outside.

"Don't listen to them, Carlos," José said, slinging one arm around Carlos's shoulder. "You're too good a dancer for that. You've got a future."

Carlos nodded. His friends understood. Inez understood. His uncle Alfonso, who wasn't allowed in the house anymore, whose success as a salsa dancer made his father sick, understood him better than anyone.

But his older brother with the hamburger franchise, and his other brother who worked at the car wash didn't; above all, his parents didn't. They each had their plans for him, and could care less about what he wanted. Carlos got into the pickup. José claimed the passenger seat; the other guys jumped into the back. Carlos could feel José looking at him. "Not to worry, *amigo,* I know exactly what I'm doing with my life," he said, and gripped the steering wheel tightly. "It isn't college. And it sure isn't welding."

But inside, he seethed. Dance was his choice. His life. He was getting sick of these fights. Almost as sick as he was of trying to get his parents to accept who he was, and what he loved.

Chapter Ten

 Laverne has perfect timing. Or *Laverne has rotten timing.* Sophy couldn't decide which.

Probably both, she reflected as she sat in the reading room of the High Falls Public Library that evening. Her mother had dropped her off an hour ago with a promise to pick her up at nine when she finished teaching her night class, and when Sophy's homework was supposed to be done. Ah, homework. Always the bane of her existence.

Sophy scribbled the word "bane" three times on the sheet of loose-leaf paper in front of her. So far her book report due tomorrow consisted of exactly six words: *Jane Austen's* Emma *is a novel.*

But how, on the night of the day when she almost had experienced her very first kiss, could a girl be expected to do homework? Half the day Sophy's feet seemed to be floating inches above the floor. The other half of the day, Sophy's heart felt like lead. She felt like a person who had suddenly been split right in two.

She was dying to see Carlos. She wished she never had to see him again. One almost kiss. One almost tango. Still, that didn't change the fact that for the most part he was a walking ego machine.

But dancing with him this morning had been, well, *romantic*. Like your basic forties movie stuff. The music, the movement of the dance, the way his touch guided her this way and that across the studio. The way he—Sophy's face went red, and she blurted right out loud, "I just can't stand it!" Then she buried her head in her arms.

"Quiet!" the librarian whispered loudly from the desk.

Sophy sat up, cheeks still scarlet, and tried to look quiet. But how could she? Inside, she was anything but. Besides, she was starving. *Starving*. Now that was a good sign. People in love lost their appetites. They never starved, unless they had a broken heart. Sophy's heart felt fine. Terrific, actually. Glowing. Happy. Like the candy-red, perfectly shaped cartoon heart on all the labels for healthy food these days. Grabbing her bag, leaving her books, she tiptoed out of the reading room.

Outside, the sky was still streaked a dirty orange and deep blue. Sophy took a deep breath and tried to locate herself. She seldom came downtown alone. To the left was the bus depot, and a row of appliance and garden supply shops, clustered at the base of one of High Falls's steep, hilly streets. To the right, High Street led down toward Main. About a block away she spotted a familiar red-and-gold awning: PATEL'S. The curry joint was cheap, fast and, conveniently, located right under Rainbow Dance.

She knew Carlos taught at night sometimes at the ballroom school. She wondered when he had a dinner break.

A few minutes later, Sophy was at the counter ordering a curry and puri special.

The screen door banged shut, and Sophy turned around. "Inez!" she said, a little let down.

"Sophy Bartlett? What are you doing here?" Inez grabbed a soda from a refrigerated case and walked up to the counter.

"My mom dumped me at the library. I'm supposed to be working, but I was starving."

"You haven't eaten yet?" Inez asked, pocketing her change.

The counter person put Sophy's order in a plastic bag. "I have," Sophy admitted. "But sometimes I get so hungry, I can eat two dinners."

"Tell me about it," Inez said, holding open the door for Sophy.

"But don't tell Daly!" Sophy warned playfully.

"She's pretty concerned about her weight. Seems silly. She looks great," Inez noted. "Hey, if you don't mind sitting on the stoop here, why don't you eat while I'm taking a break." Inez motioned with her head toward the stairs leading up the outside of the building to the dance studio. "It's hot up there. Classes aren't too crowded tonight. No one will miss me for a while."

On the chance Carlos might come downstairs for air, Sophy agreed readily.

"So how did rehearsal go today with you guys and Laverne?"

"Oh, haven't you seen Carlos?" Sophy asked, smoothing a napkin over her short cotton miniskirt and feeling a pang of disappointment.

"Not to speak to. We have different schedules in school. He was here earlier for his lesson. Mrs. Ivanov really laid into him and Roxanna. *¡Ay!* You should have seen it. She was absolutely *loco* tonight."

"Roxanna?"

"That, too, but it was her mother." Inez laughed a throaty laugh. For a small girl her voice was unusually rich and deep. "Most of us have bad-hair days. Roxanna has bad *dance* days."

Sophy cracked up, suddenly looking at Inez in a new light. She seemed shy, but beneath that demure exterior lurked a girl with some of Carlos's edge.

"So what happened to Carlos?" Sophy asked.

Inez shrugged. "Guess he went home. I didn't see him after La Ivanov kicked him out. Something about him turning into an inconsiderate or sloppy partner." Inez grew thoughtful. "Weird, no matter what's going on with him, he's never that."

Was it possible? Was Carlos as rattled by this morning as she'd been? Had it actually affected his *dancing?* Sophy indulged the thought. Then pictured Carlos. Nah. One thing she was sure of. Whatever happened in his life, he never would let his dancing suffer. She suspected when it came to his dedication to dance, they could be twins.

"Roxanna, on the other hand . . . "

"She's more uneven?" Sophy suggested, packing up the rest of her food to save for lunch.

"No—but today, well, she sort of looked wiped out. And I heard her mother yell at her after Carlos left. She said something about a dancer needing her rest. Her mother was accusing her of partying too much. I didn't really hear more than that. They switched to Russian."

Inez pitched her soda can into one of the city recycling baskets along the curb. She got up and stretched her arms over her head. "But you never told me what happened at Laverne's practice this morning."

"Laverne never showed—or almost never. She turned up over an hour late, with the flu. We postponed the whole thing." Sophy stopped there. If Carlos hadn't mentioned her tango lesson to Inez, she'd just as soon keep it private.

Above them the windows of the dance studio were open. Strains of music floated out into the street. It sounded familiar to Sophy. "That's a tango."

"Yeah," Inez said. They both listened. "That's one of the classic Argentinean bands of the forties. Here, let me show you how it's danced."

Sophy hesitated.

"Come on, I won't bite!" Inez teased. "Besides, I'm learning to lead it. Women dance instructors have to learn to lead as well as follow."

Inez put one hand on Sophy's waist. Sophy automatically clasped her other hand the way Carlos had shown her just that morning. Inez was a little shorter than Sophy, but she was a strong lead. They danced a few steps down the sidewalk.

Sophy felt like Gene Kelly sashaying down the street in *Singing in the Rain*. She half expected a camera to materialize on the corner of Tower and Main, and someone to yell, "Cut."

Instead, as they landed back at the foot of the stairs, Inez was yelling, "I don't believe it. *I do not believe it!* You've been studying with Carlos!" She sounded amazed, and a little left out.

Sophy turned red, but it was dark except for the streetlights, and she knew Inez couldn't tell she was blushing. She covered her own confusion with a laugh. "It's not what you think," she said hurriedly. *Or was it?*

"Sophy Bartlett, what's going on here?" Inez gazed at her with frank curiosity.

"Nothing, as in NOT A THING. When Laverne didn't show, Carlos decided I needed to learn to tango. 'The right way'!" Sophy darkened her voice and imitated Carlos's swagger.

Inez giggled. "That's my brother. Still, you're a really quick study," she complimented her.

Sophy had a funny feeling Inez didn't quite believe her. It really had been only one lesson. Just this morning.

At the sound of approaching footsteps, both girls turned. A forty-something-year-old guy was walking up the hill from Main toward them. He had scruffy blondish hair, a weathered face, and a limp that made Sophy ache to watch him walk.

"Oh, Mikhail!" Inez cried warmly. She hurried down the block to meet him, taking some of his packages. She slowed her pace to match his as they neared Sophy. "Sophy, this is him. This is my teacher. Roxanna's father. Mikhail Ivanov."

"Hello, Mr. Ivanov. I'm Sophy. Sophy Bartlett. I go to the Ballet Academy."

"The Academy?" he repeated, looking interested. "You are student there?" His heavy accent made him sound a little severe, but there was something kind about his eyes. He turned to Inez. "What time is it? Should you be home soon?"

Inez checked her watch. "Oh, it's late!" she cried, and shot Sophy an apologetic look. "I didn't mean to hang out here so long. Now the library's going to close and you haven't gotten back to your homework."

"Not to worry," Sophy confided. Thinking of *Singing in the Rain* had inspired her. "I haven't even read the book I'm supposed to be writing about. But I don't have to. I'll just take the video out of the library tonight and write a couple of pages before bed. But I'd better get back to the library before it closes."

"Are you going far?" Mikhail asked Sophy. She

explained that her mother would be giving her a ride home. He started for the stairs, then turned around. "The Academy, it is not a big school?"

Sophy shook her head.

"You know a young black girl? She is tall, about your age, maybe a little older?"

"Laverne," Sophy declared.

"Laverne," Inez stated. "She's the mastermind behind our fund-raiser. The girl I told you about."

"Yes," he said, "the choreographer."

"Why?" Sophy asked, but Mikhail had turned away and was slowly walking up the stairs. Inez shrugged at Sophy, then gave her a little wave before disappearing into the building behind him.

Sophy waved back, wondering, what was this about Laverne?

♡   ♡   ♡

The bass was pumped up. The tin roof of the colorful building vibrated to the beat. Milongas's salsa night was in high gear. But Carlos stood outside the club in Payner's Alley, leaning back against the cool clapboards. He was so lonely, his soul actually ached.

For the first time in his life dancing had let him down. Always, before tonight, he could lose himself in the beat of the music. Salsa especially never had failed to cheer him right up.

Tonight, the joyful noise turned him right off.

Weird, though. The fights at home had often been worse. Much, much worse. This time it wasn't between him and his father. It was between his parents. The old College versus Tech School debate. That's what came of being not just a good dancer, but a straight-A student. Carlos believed in throwing himself wholeheartedly, body and soul, into anything he tackled.

So what had happened to him today? Where had all of his strength and determination gone when Mrs. Ivanov had started in? Or when he had Sophy in his arms? Just thinking about her, suddenly Carlos didn't feel strong at all. He just felt lonely and seventeen.

Misunderstood youth. Let's be James Dean tonight. Let's be a rebel.

Somehow the image didn't quite fit. Rebels died in movies. They had sad lives. They were often failures. Rebels weren't ballroom dancing champions.

"Carlos? You out there, man?" José called, poking his head outside. "The band's tuning up. Live music hour's about to start. Some of the girls from school are here. Everyone's asking for you."

"In that case," Carlos forced a laugh, "I wouldn't want to disappoint them—especially those girls. Be right in."

His comeback sounded a little hollow. Tonight was not a night for dancing or for girls, he thought as he followed José back inside. But moping wasn't going to solve anything. He might as well enjoy the band.

As he passed the phone booth, he suddenly knew

exactly what he had to do. José and the guys were great, but they weren't dancers.

He dug in his pocket for a quarter. He dialed home. Inez should be back from Rainbow Dance by now. Just before the first ring, he hung up. What if his parents answered? Besides, maybe it wasn't such a good idea to get Inez involved in this latest round of the family feud.

What if their dad got mad at her and pulled the plug on her dance career just as it was about to take off in new directions? No, he couldn't involve Inez. Not this time.

Of course there was someone else. The one person he'd met outside of Inez whose passion for dance equaled his own. He didn't know her number. But her address would be somewhere not far from here. There couldn't be too many Bartletts in the neighborhood of the university. He started to dial directory assistance. Then pressed down the receiver.

Was he nuts? What made him think Sophy really would stop long enough to give him the time of day? Sure, they'd actually managed to spend one practice together, barely fighting. Big deal. What made him think she'd stoop low enough to hang out with him, outside of school?

The way she looked at you, a voice inside reminded him. They had just finished dancing— one minute, standing in her toe shoes, she was exactly his height; the next she was off pointe. He had to look down a little to find her. She was still looking up at him, a surprised smile on those beautiful lips. Waiting to be kissed.

Or had that just been his imagination? Thanks to Laverne's bummed-out timing, he'd never know for sure now.

"Look who's here!" A pretty blonde poked her face right under his. "How come you're hogging the phone? How come the king of the salsa scene isn't dancing?"

"Daly?" Carlos grinned to see her. Daly was always sunny and cheerful—and always put him in an upbeat mood. "I was outside," he said. "Getting air."

"Where's Roxanna?" P. J. asked. Carlos let himself be herded with the group away from the phone and into the main room of the club.

P. J. was with a girl. Not Sophy. Not his partner, but a girl he'd seen him around with before.

"And Inez?" Ray asked, looking behind Carlos. "What's she up to?"

Carlos threw up his hands and laughed. Just the act of laughing made him feel better. "I don't travel with a whole entourage. Though you guys seem to." He surveyed the small group of kids: Lara, from homeroom at school; Academy students; P. J. and his girl. His hopes lifted, then fell. Everyone but Sophy seemed to be there.

Chapter Eleven

Is this the real life of Laverne Theresa Grey? It was four days before the gala, and Laverne was beginning to wonder if she were living a dream. The newly formed student committee was meeting with the school directors in the top floor music room in the north wing of the building. The sound of hammering, sawing, and sanding filtered up from the studios below, where renovation of the studios for Rainbow Dance had already started. To Laverne, the thumps and bangs and voices of the workmen sounded like music. The day Carlos Vargas suggested this merger was the luckiest of Laverne's life.

She sat on the edge of her chair, feeling better than she had about herself since—since she couldn't say when. The business meeting was over, and it was Laverne's turn to take the floor. The Laverne she used to be wouldn't be caught dead on a school committee, let alone be the head of one.

But for the first time in her life, and thanks to Sophy's backing during the planning session for the fund-raiser, Laverne was in charge of something and she loved it.

"So, Laverne, how's the gala shaping up?" Peter

MacGregor asked, propping his elbows on the card table set up in the Academy's small music studio. Along with Peter, his wife, Jan, and Nadia Ivanov were there. Roxanna's father hadn't turned up yet.

Laverne sat a little straighter. "Great," she said. "Everyone's been working hard, making it to rehearsals in spite of the rushed schedule; WHF-TV is sending a crew to the performance, and the *Herald*'s arts critic called for press seats—thanks to Daly, Ray, and Inez." Laverne looked across the room and flashed the trio a smile.

Funny how in just a couple of weeks, kids from the two schools were beginning to hang out together, and friendships were forming. Even Sophy and Carlos were able to work together on this committee, as well as rehearse, without too much fighting. And somehow Laverne had become part of the group. This was a new feeling, not being an outsider. Laverne, the loose cannon, the troublemaker. All that talent and no discipline. Forever, people had told her that.

She knew the other students thought she was only in the MacGregors's advanced class because of her famous father. Until now she hadn't realized how lonely she'd felt being "the Academy's Rebel in Residence."

"Has anything happened about the name for the school?" Sophy asked. She was sitting with Shanti, across from Roxanna and Carlos.

Laverne caught Roxanna's eye, and her smile

broadened into a grin. "Inspiration has struck again—"

A chorus of groans rose from the kids. Peter laughed. Nadia looked puzzled, Jan, worried.

Roxanna preened. Laverne waited until the room quieted, then went on. "But this time credit goes to Roxanna. It's her idea; let her tell you about it."

"It's not that big a deal, really," Roxanna said with a modest smile. "I just figured we should have a contest. Whoever comes up with the name the board chooses wins a prize. I thought we should open the contest to anyone in High Falls under the age of eighteen. That way, we get local kids involved. And the prize can be a month of free dance classes—ballroom and ballet, at the school."

"That's great!" Carlos exclaimed.

"It'll be free publicity at the same time," Daly complimented her.

But before anyone could say more, the door opened and a slender man limped in. "I am late. Sorry, I was caught in traffic downtown," the man said with a heavy accent. A familiar accent, Laverne realized. Where had she heard it before?

"Mikhail, welcome!" Peter got up and shook the man's hand. "Does everyone here know Mikhail Ivanov, the codirector of Rainbow Dance and the fifth member of the board of directors here?"

So this was Roxanna's mysterious father. Laverne smiled at him. He didn't smile back. *What's his problem?* she wondered, catching

Roxanna's eye. Roxanna gave a quick small shake of her head, then put her finger to her lips as if warning Laverne about something.

Of course! Laverne realized—the other night. As if she could forget the mess at Tangos and Sauce. The fight had even made the local evening news, but luckily the next day a scandal about the mayor had broken, making everyone forget about the fight and the "underage girls" who supposedly had caused it. Laverne looked at Roxanna now and nodded, to show she understood. No way would she want to get her new friend in trouble with her dad.

"That more or less wraps business up today," Peter was saying as he gathered some papers and started to get up from the table. Mr. Ivanov put his hand on Peter's arm and made him sit down again. Peter continued to smile at Laverne. "And thanks, Laverne, for all your good work."

Beaming, Laverne got up, tugged down the back of her leotard, and yanked up her red leg warmers. "Thank you, Peter," she said, adding to herself, *for trusting me with this.*

"Okay, crew," she said to the other kids."Let's head for Studio B and another run-through."

Halfway out the door, Peter called her back. "Laverne, I need to talk to you."

Laverne turned. Peter was frowning. "Uh— sure," she said, stepping back into the room. "Sophy," she called, sticking her head out the door, "can you take the rehearsal until I get there?"

What's wrong with this picture? Roxanna asked herself half an hour later. *Everything!* she answered herself glumly.

She was sick of cooling her heels. Her *high* black heels, which made her feet ache. She hated waiting to rehearse Laverne's take on the Black Swan pas de deux with P. J. while watching as Sophy Bartlett dug her claws a little deeper into Carlos. That girl wasn't just a snob, she was a real operator when it came to guys. She came off all cold and innocent, one of those "dance is my life" types. What a sham! *She even had me fooled,* Roxanna realized, disgusted with herself.

But she had to admit, if Carlos weren't Sophy's target, she would actually admire the girl's con.

Studio A, on the second floor of the Ballet Academy, was large: at least twice as large as the biggest studio at Rainbow Dance. But Roxanna decided it wasn't big enough to hold her and Sophy.

Watching her tango in those dumb pink toe shoes, clinging to Carlos like a vine, turned Roxanna's stomach. When she couldn't take even one more second of the disgusting display, Roxanna marched over to the little alcove beside the studio door and flicked off the tape.

Carlos cursed in Spanish.

Sophy turned and glared at Roxanna.

Roxanna glared back. "Sophy, you're supposed to be running the rehearsal, not *hogging* it!"

"I'm not hogging anything, Roxanna," Sophy countered, her big gray eyes narrowing like a cat's. "If you don't believe me, look at Laverne's notes. First Ray and Daly do their pas de deux; then Aiko and Ray practice their ballet salsa number. Next, me and Carlos. You and P. J. come afterward." Roxanna could practically feel Sophy grit her teeth. "You just have to wait your turn," Sophy concluded, striding over to the tape machine.

Roxanna planted herself in front of the console and blocked her way. "In a ballroom studio, we *share* the music. One couple uses their music for a while, then another changes to theirs. We switch back and forth."

"In case you haven't noticed, this isn't a ballroom studio!" Sophy retorted, pushing behind Roxanna to turn on the tape.

"Come off it, Sophy." Carlos sounded exasperated. "I thought we were past all that! We're one school now."

"*This* is not about the school, Carlos. It's about having less than three whole days to rehearse, with a major gala coming up," Sophy declared, sounding a little hysterical.

"Time out!" P. J. said, stepping between Carlos, Sophy, and Roxanna. He put his hand on Roxanna's shoulder. "Roxy's just eager to go through our routine. But, really, we've all got to learn to work together. That's what part of this fund-raiser's about, at least for me."

"Me too," Daly spoke up. "But Sophy's right on one point. Time's running out. I'm getting awfully nervous about this gala. Like cable is actually going to be filming part of the performance to show on the news. I'll die if we look like some kind of little kids' school recital."

"Well, we won't look like that. Not with this cast." P. J. laughed. He pushed his thick blond hair off his forehead and turned to Roxanna. "Let's just let Sophy and Carlos run through their piece one more time."

Of course he'd stick up for her, Roxanna thought bitterly, but she smiled her most gracious warm smile and leaned into P. J. She looked up at him with wide eyes. "You've got a point," she said sweetly. But when Sophy turned on the music and headed back to Carlos, Roxanna had to turn around. She couldn't bear watching them dance together anymore. And she vowed to herself that somehow she'd make sure that after this gala they'd never dance together again.

The music had barely started when it stopped again.

"Roxanna!" Carlos yelled, pushing Sophy aside and turning toward the door. His face shifted from anger to surprise.

Roxanna wasn't even near the tape deck. She followed Carlos's gaze. "Mr. MacGregor?" He had his hand on the tape recorder. Roxanna spied her mother just inside the open door. Her mother looked livid.

Behind her mother was a tall, light-skinned black man. *Laverne's father?!* The famous Edmund Grey. She'd never even seen him before, but he had Laverne's straight nose and chiseled cheekbones. Roxanna shrank back against the barre.

Laverne. That little snitch! was her first thought. Her second was to find the fire escape and make a fast exit. She was actually eyeing the open window when Sophy broke the strained silence.

"Peter? What's wrong? We were just rehearsing, and . . ." Sophy seemed to notice the tall black man for the first time. The look of confusion on her face turned to worry. "Has something happened to Laverne, Mr. Grey?"

Laverne's father exchanged a glance with Peter, but didn't reply to Sophy.

Peter motioned Nadia and the other man inside the studio, then closed the door behind them. "No, Sophy, not exactly. Nothing's *happened* to Laverne that she didn't bring on herself. Apparently she's one of the girls, the *underage* girls," he stressed, "that was on the scene of that bar brawl last week."

"More precisely," Edmund Grey said coolly, "one of the girls who started the fight."

"Brawl?" Sophy gasped.

"What brawl?" Roxanna managed to sound suitably stunned. Was it possible? Had Laverne really not spilled the beans? Had she left Roxanna out of it? Roxanna cast a sidelong glance at her mother. If her mother knew already, why was she looking daggers at every other girl in the room?

"Down at Tangos and Sauce." Everyone turned and gaped at Carlos.

"*You* were there?" Nadia's shock shifted to an I-told-you-so sort of tone. "Though why *that* should surprise me . . ." She shrugged, then turned to Peter. Roxanna took a step forward into the room. *No. Not Carlos. He wasn't there. I know. Don't lay into him now.* But she pursed her lips. She couldn't afford to give herself away like that. Somehow she'd make it up to him when this blew over.

"I wasn't there," Carlos said, offended. "Not that night. I hang there sometimes with friends. It's a good salsa club. My uncle plays there when he's in town. As for the brawl, I heard about it around school or wherever. Everyone knows. I just can't imagine Laverne being involved. She doesn't even look eighteen, really."

"Apparently she looked close enough to twenty-one to fool the ticket takers that night. Anyway, Carlos, we'll just have to believe you weren't there. We do know that one other girl was with Laverne that night. Until we find out which one of you that was," Peter said sternly, "there will be no more rehearsals for the fund-raiser—"

"But Peter," Sophy cried, "everything's still so rough. We *need* to rehearse, and—"

"Enough, Sophy!" Peter raised his voice. "Believe me, rehearsals are beside the point. Unless we find out who was with Laverne at the club that night, there will be no fund-raiser."

"No fund-raiser!?" Sophy gasped.

"That's not fair!" Daly cried.

"But the schools need the money, and the press is coming, and—" Inez burst out.

"Laverne didn't tell you who was with her," Ray stated quietly. Roxanna could hear the respect in his voice. She realized all the other kids felt the same way, too. Whatever Peter threatened, no one liked the idea of a tattletale. On her part, Roxanna didn't care much about respect; she was just really, really grateful that Laverne could keep her mouth shut. Still, she wanted to be extra sure.

"Besides, Mr. MacGregor," Roxanna spoke up. As soon as she got his attention, she looked around the room. "What makes you think it's a girl from here? I mean, Laverne has other friends she hangs with, I'm sure. No Academy girl would go to a place like that. As for those of us from Rainbow Dance . . ." Roxanna looked offended. "None of us would dare!" She met her mother's eyes, and relief washed over her. Her mother actually looked a little proud.

"Roxanna, maybe you wouldn't go to that sort of place, but we are pretty sure someone from here did," Nadia said.

Edmund Grey spoke up. "Kids at the club told police that both girls who crashed the gate that night were very good dancers. They looked professional, is what one young man said."

"The police?" Roxanna's voice went weak.

"Laverne's going to be arrested?" Sophy's hands flew to her mouth.

"No. The girls did nothing wrong, except lie about their age. The police can't even hold the club responsible, because they have no proof. And fortunately that brawl never escalated to the point that someone got seriously hurt. A few fines and community service work took care of the guys involved."

"So then, what's the big deal here?" Carlos asked.

"The big deal, Carlos Vargas," Nadia fumed, "is that this school—both schools—won't tolerate criminals."

"Laverne's no criminal," Sophy spoke up, and all the other kids assented loudly.

"No, she's not. But she did break the law," her father said. "She's got to learn her lesson."

"You're kicking her out of the school?" Shanti spoke up, shaken.

"This time, no," Peter stated. "She's grounded. She's on probation."

A sigh of relief circled the room. "But what if you don't find out who was with her? What if it really wasn't anyone here?" Sophy asked.

"Laverne has some crazy idea she's helping someone by keeping her mouth shut," her father said. "All she's doing is possibly jeopardizing the future of the school."

"That's not fair," several voices cried.

"Mother, don't tell me you're going along with this?" Roxanna asked. This was too much pressure for Laverne. She'd be sure to give in, thinking her own dance career was at stake. In her shoes, Roxanna sure would.

Nadia just shrugged.

Peter held up his hand, and the room fell silent. "The bottom line is that unless Laverne wises up and stops playing the hero—or unless whoever was with her has the courage to speak up—the performance will be canceled."

Chapter Twelve

The door slammed shut behind Peter. For a heartbeat the studio was still as stone. Then everyone began talking at once.

"Why did Laverne have to pull a dumb stunt like this? Why now?" Carlos fumed. He started toward the dressing room. He was so bummed out, he just wanted to change and get out of here.

Ray tossed down his towel. "This time Laverne's gone too far."

"Meaning?" Roxanna said, tapping her high-heeled foot against the floor. "Would you be happy if she had snitched on her pal?"

"No!" Ray countered, giving Roxanna a look of pure disgust. "Of course not."

Daly put her hand on Ray's arm. "Meaning, Roxanna, that Laverne always manages to get into some kind of trouble."

"You guys knew this?" Aiko exclaimed. "So how come she was put in charge?"

"Wasn't it Sophy's idea?" Roxanna suggested. Her snide tone snapped Carlos out of his funk. Had the Queen of Jealousy somehow psyched out his feelings for Sophy? Sophy sure hadn't, he thought, casting a quick glance in her direction. Sophy looked dejected, distant. The way her face sort of closed down when she was upset intrigued him. She was so different from himself, from Inez, from other people he loved. *Loved?* What in the world was he thinking? His life was falling apart, and he was in dreamland. He hadn't even kissed the girl. He wasn't even sure they were friends!

Friends or not, he couldn't let Roxanna put her down. Before he could say anything, Sophy jumped to her own defense.

"No," Sophy protested. "Laverne volunteered to organize the show. I just said she'd be good at it. And she is—or was. . . ." Sophy floundered and, for a moment, her armor cracked. She looked like she was about to cry.

Carlos couldn't stand it. "In charge or not," he interjected quickly, "that isn't the point. Peter would have canceled the fund-raiser no matter who was running it. He's just pressuring whoever was with Laverne to speak up. He's trying to force her hand." Carlos shrugged. "He might as well cancel the gala now. No one here would tell on a friend."

Everyone nodded. P. J. grabbed his towel from the barre and said, "I couldn't live with myself if *I* turned someone in, but whoever was with Laverne should own up to it herself. Laverne shouldn't be put in this position."

For a moment no one spoke up. None of the girls met each other's eyes. Carlos looked at each one in turn: Daly, Inez, Roxanna, Aiko, Shanti—the group of soloists slated to be at that day's rehearsal. Last of all he looked at Sophy. Except for Roxy, none of these girls looked sophisticated enough—or even interested enough for the club scene. Except for Daly, as far as he knew none of them were even really dating yet.

Roxanna—she was another animal entirely. She made no secret of liking guys, and her parents didn't know half of what went on in her social life, though Carlos had heard a few things around the school. Nothing definite, nothing really bad, but still . . . he scrutinized her beautiful face. One smile from those full red full lips and bouncers would let her walk all over them.

Forget it, Vargas! Carlos told himself. Roxanna Ivanov was too ambitious to waste her time crashing clubs and drinking. She'd never open herself up to any kind of serious trouble. She had her eye on the Olympics. Scandal was not in Roxanna's scheme of things.

Turning to Sophy, he said, "But that explains why she stood us up at rehearsal that morning. That was the day the news broke about the brawl at Tangos and Sauce."

Sophy stared blankly at Carlos, then she made a face. "Am I jerk of the year, or what?!" She laughed tightly. "Remember, I even told her she looked like a commercial for a hangover remedy."

Carlos shrugged and felt sheepish. "More like I was the jerk here. I told you she probably had the flu. It really was a hangover."

"Laverne Grey was *drinking?*" Daly gasped. "No wonder her dad is so mad! He must be furious. Wouldn't want to be in her shoes right now. She'll be grounded for months!"

"We don't know that for sure about the drinking," Carlos pointed out. "But I bet that's why Peter's being so hard-nosed about the whole thing. Word must have gotten out that the girls in the club that night were drinking."

"Hard to believe they'd fool the staff at Tangos and Sauce. That club is pretty decent. Things get rowdy now and then, but it's not a dive." P. J. looked to Carlos for confirmation. "You've been there, Carlos, when your uncle played there."

"Yeah. He got me in, but had to swear in fifteen different languages that I'd stick to soda." Carlos scratched his head thoughtfully. "They really card people in a big way. I still can't believe Laverne passed for twenty-one. She looks *so* young."

All the girls in the room groaned. "Sometimes guys are so dense," Daly said, giggling.

"Hey girls, this guy hasn't ever heard of makeup, as in M-A-K-E-U-P." Roxanna spelled the words out. She treated Carlos to a look of mock disgust. Then she lifted her shoulders. "I've passed for over twenty-one myself on occasion," she said.

Her words hung in the air a second. Everyone was gaping at Roxanna. Carlos caught his breath. Sure, Roxanna had definitely passed for over twenty-one. He'd been with her once. They had made the rounds of some salsa clubs down in Philadelphia after a competition last spring. They both had sailed past the checkers at the door. Dressed up, Carlos came off much older than most guys his age, too.

Roxanna caught his eye; for a moment she seemed to be pleading with him to keep his mouth shut. Then she tossed back her hair and said to the crowd, "Now don't look at me! I was just pointing out that I, like everyone else here, can look older if I try to. That doesn't mean I was at Tangos and Sauce the other night. In fact," she added, "where is that joint, anyway? I thought I knew all the Latin clubs in town."

"It's new. It opened last month, down by the university," Carlos answered, ready to kick himself for even remotely suspecting Roxanna of stooping so low—leaving Laverne in the lurch like that.

"Oh! That's in your neighborhood, Sophy," Roxanna said in an insinuating tone.

Carlos stiffened. Sophy paled. "So? Lots of clubs are in my neighborhood. I only live one block up the hill from University and Canal Streets. That doesn't mean I go to them. I've never been to Tangos and Sauce," Sophy informed Roxanna curtly. To make herself perfectly clear, she added, "To any club, ever, in any neighborhood, not even yours."

"Sophy wasn't there," Carlos said, absolutely sure of that. Taking a walk on the wild side wasn't Sophy's style.

"How do you know?" Roxanna narrowed her

eyes. "Were you with her? Rehearsing all night—or something?"

Carlos's stomach clenched. The girl was going too far. "Maybe. Maybe not." He leveled his gaze at Roxanna, but avoided Sophy's eyes.

"Carlos?" Sophy cried, offended and shocked. "You know perfectly well we weren't—"

Daly didn't let her finish. "Wherever you were or weren't, it's no one's business—unless it was the club, and you weren't there. Don't let her get to you."

"Stop it, everybody," Inez broke in, her voice trembling. "We can't start accusing each other of all sorts of stuff."

"Each other?" Sophy cried, wrapping her arms tightly around her chest. "Seems Roxanna's pointing the finger at me."

"She's just jealous that you're dancing with Carlos for the show." Inez put her arm around Sophy. Silently, Carlos blessed his sister for that.

"Doesn't she wish." Roxanna shrugged. "You couldn't pay me to dance in that dumb 'Tangos and Tutus' number Laverne cooked up."

"Funny," Daly commented. "I recall you volunteered for the job—something about having studied pointe a few years ago."

"Time out, girls!" P. J. commanded, and cast a pleading look at Carlos. With a slight bend of his head, he gestured toward the tape deck. "Peter hasn't kicked us out or anything. I say we get on with this rehearsal—"

178 *heart beats*

Voices began to protest. But Carlos picked up P. J.'s theme. "He's right. For all we know, Peter is bluffing—"

"Right," Ray scoffed.

"But if he is, Ray, we aren't in any kind of shape to put on a show. I suggest we finish our run-through, and maybe P. J., since he's the most senior student here, can take over the rehearsal," Carlos added, then braved Sophy's eyes as he reached for her clipboard. She might hate him for this. But for the sake of peace, he'd risk it.

She flashed him a look of pure gratitude. "Thanks," she said so softly, he barely caught it. Louder, she added, "Good idea. I'm not good at directing something and dancing at the same time."

"Me either, so I'm going to wait this one out. Roxanna and I can work on our bit later," P. J. said, then quickly perused Laverne's notes. "Since we've had a long break here, I suggest the ballet people warm up again, at the barre on the far end of the room. That shouldn't interfere with the ballroom numbers. Okay, Sophy?" he asked.

"Hey, it's your call!" she said, sounding gracious and relieved.

Carlos watched her cross the room, pull on nylon warm-up pants over her tights, and adjust her hair in the mirror. She suddenly looked so small, so fragile, he wanted to go right up to her and hold her and tell her everything would be all right. He took one step in her direction.

"We're on!" Roxanna said, her hand closing lightly around his wrist. "Inez and Nick; Aiko and Tommy are waiting."

"Right, that waltz," Carlos said, reeling his thoughts back from Sophy. He took Roxanna's hand and struggled to regain his poise, his posture. The luscious Viennese music swelled through the studio. For a second it seemed his feet were glued to the floor. Across the room was the girl who made him feel like waltzing. In his arms was a girl he was beginning to wish he'd never met. Years of training, a zillion or so hours of rehearsing, rescued him. He put one hand around Roxanna's trim waist, and held her other hand. He put on his best romantic smile, and waltzed counterclockwise around the room. Inez and Will on one side of them and Aiko and Tommy Mintz on the other. He and Roxanna glided like one body through the dance. *One body,* he silently told Sophy as he passed her warming up at the barre, *but not one heart.*

♡   ♡   ♡

"Just because Laverne's a loser, Peter has no right to punish the rest of us!" Sophy exclaimed, slamming the dishwasher door shut. She and Emma were in their grandparents' kitchen that evening, helping clear the dinner things. Sophy's grandparents lived right next door, in the other side of the huge two-family house they all shared. When their mother taught evenings, the girls often ate with their grandparents.

Earlier, Sophy had told her grandmother everything—well, almost everything—about the blowup at school, and Peter's threats to cancel the fund-raiser. She had decided not to mention the matter of Laverne's underage drinking. "It's gruesome, totally gruesome, Grams!" she concluded now.

"More like awesome!" Emma contradicted, putting away her dish towel and settling into a chair. "The way you're freaked out about this. Seems about two weeks ago you were ready to run away from home rather than set foot in the new school."

Sophy's grandmother laughed and leaned back against the counter. She regarded Sophy with her big gray eyes full of sparkle. Lara Giraud, Sophy's mother's mom, was an elegant-looking slender woman with salt-and-pepper gray hair and whom Sophy resembled slightly. "Seems like Laverne gave you the way out."

"That was *then*. This is *now*," Sophy retorted curtly, then noticed the twinkle in her grandmother's eyes. "Stop teasing me," she ordered, but cracked a small smile.

"I'm curious, Sudsy," her grandmother said, dropping back to Sophy's childhood nickname. When Emma was little, "Sophy" was too hard for her to say, so Emma took to calling her Soaps, which the rest of the family turned to Sudsy. Sophy hated it now when anyone but Grams called her that. "What brought about this change of mind?"

"Who's changed their mind?" Sophy said. She

moving as one 181

sat on the window seat in the breakfast nook and drew her knees up to her chest. She was wearing a big roomy shirt over her tank top and jeans. A cool draft blew through the window. She tucked her hands inside the deep pockets and leaned against the wall. "I still think it's a mistake to combine ballet and ballroom. But it's the best solution for now. I wish it were a temporary thing. It's not. And there's not much I can do to stop it. I only wish things could go back to what they were last year, with the Academy just the Academy—no money problems, and no ballroom stuff attached."

"There's nothing wrong with ballroom," said her grandmother, putting the kettle on the stove. "Your father was a pretty terrific ballroom dancer."

"What!!!" Sophy cried, feeling as if someone had punched her in the stomach.

"Get outta here!" Emma gasped. "Grams, you're making that up!"

Their grandmother laughed and shrugged. "Now why would I do that?"

Emma's answer was instant. "To make Sophy feel better."

"Better about what?" Sophy said, a bitter taste in her mouth. She regarded her grandmother and felt betrayed. "You're getting just like Mom. Doling out Dad by dribs and drabs."

Her grandmother's expression softened. "Suds, stop it. You know that's not what's going on. Your mother—well, she finds it hard to talk about him.

Imagine what it's like to wake up one morning and find your husband is gone."

"She must have seen it coming," Sophy said, but grew thoughtful. The man-woman thing—the stuff between girls and guys, even—it was all so confusing. What were men all about? Who knew what went on inside their heads? Take Carlos. A few days ago he had almost kissed her. Since then—nothing. Of course they hadn't had a minute alone. Rehearsing with the whole cast day after day. But even when they were dancing, he was cool, all business. As if that morning in the studio simply hadn't happened.

Then this afternoon: One minute he was rushing to her defense, the next—Sophy's heart hardened just thinking of it—the next he was waltzing across the floor with Roxanna, lost in those big sloe eyes, looking as if he were ready to dance her right into the sunset. Sophy had felt hurt, lonely, and really bad. Could her mother have been just as confused by her dad?

"No. She didn't see it coming, Sophy. Your mother had no idea. Not at all."

Sophy looked up, startled. "I thought maybe they'd been fighting and stuff"—Sophy stopped—"but I would have remembered that," she realized, as the kettle began to whistle.

"But what's this about him dancing? Did he go to Rainbow Dance like Sophy's new friends?" Emma asked, changing the subject. Sophy exchanged a glance with her grandmother. Emma always changed the subject when anyone tried to talk about why their dad had left.

Lara laughed and paused to pour water into a ceramic teapot. "Silly girl. Of course not. The Ivanovs were probably still in Leningrad—rather, Saint Petersburg—when your father was dancing. That was back in the nineteen seventies."

"He studied ballroom?" Sophy was suddenly curious and confused. How could Mom not have told her this?

"Never. Not a lesson in his life. Not at that point. But he was our local John Travolta."

"Like in *Saturday Night Fever*? He danced like that?" Emma gasped, sitting on the edge of her chair. She wrapped a strand of her long blond hair around her finger and gaped up at her grandmother. *Poor kid,* Sophy thought, wondering if Emma still blamed herself for her parents' breakup. She had been only a little over a year old when it had happened. But when she was old enough to understand her father had left not long after she was born, she had decided that she was the reason he'd gone.

Sophy got up and squeezed next to Emma on the chair. "Hey, stop pushing!" Emma complained, but leaned into Sophy's arm.

Their grandmother brought over the teapot and some mugs. While the tea brewed she sat across from the girls and picked up her story. "No, he didn't dance *exactly* like Travolta, but he was pretty good.

It was the height of the disco era. And he won a few local contests, including some lessons in a ballroom school over in Blairstown."

"So he studied there, then," Sophy marveled. How could her mother never have mentioned this? In her Mom's shoes she would have told Sophy about her father's dancing lessons, to try to win her over to the idea of Rainbow Dance merging with the Academy.

"I think he took one class, and then"—her grandmother's proud reminiscent tone suddenly shifted—"then he met your mother, and they got married," she concluded abruptly.

"But what about Aunt Sophy?" Emma asked suddenly. "I thought she was the dancer in family, not our Dad."

"Aunt *Sophia,*" their grandmother corrected. Her high-cheekboned face lifted into a smile. "She hated being called Sophy," she added, casting an apologetic look at Sophy. "But your mother certainly gave you the right name, Sophy. Your aunt would be so proud to see you dance."

Sophy sighed. She poured some tea into a mug and went back to the window seat. She tried to picture her aunt. No matter how hard she tried, she couldn't. There were family photos, of course, but Sophy couldn't ever remember having seen her in person. Though once she thought she remembered the smell of lilies in the winter in her room. Her mother had told her then that Aunt Sophia had baby-sat her and that the scent was her aunt's perfume. "How come I don't remember her, Grams?"

"You were too young," her grandmother replied, tracing the flowered pattern on the green-and-white-checkered tablecloth. "She wasn't around much after your parents got married. By the time you were born she was traveling with different modern dance troupes around the country. Going from city to city. She'd turn up on holidays, but it was hard for her, living on the road."

"How come she doesn't turn up now?" Emma asked, spooning honey into her tea.

"She stopped coming back. Suddenly there were no more cards, no phone calls. She dropped out of sight."

"Just like that?" Sophy asked, though she knew the story well. It always amazed her how people you loved could somehow suddenly vanish without a trace. It amazed her more that no one ever had tried to find her aunt.

"Just like that." Lara stared into her mug. As Sophy watched, her expression hardened.

Sophy pursed her lips. *What was with these people?* she wondered. Her mother clammed up about her dad. Her grandmother always cut the conversations about Aunt Sophia off. Why was her family so hush-hush about the past?

Lara got up and pushed in her chair. "I'm going to bring your grandfather some tea. He's still working in his studio," she said, looking at the clock. She filled a mug and put in honey and milk. As she started for the door, she said tightly, "I'm sorry, Sophy, about the mess at the school. You probably won't understand this now, but looking back, you'll see Peter is right. Laverne thinks she's being noble not telling on a friend. But what she's really doing is hurting the school and jeopardizing her own future. Without the gala, the new school will miss a chance for some top publicity and exposure, and who knows what kind of donations and support that might have brought in?"

"Would you tell, Grams, if you were Laverne Grey?" Emma asked.

Their grandmother paused at the door. With a rueful smile she answered, "At Sophy's age, no; but now I know better. By keeping her mouth shut, Laverne is really hurting, not helping, her friends."

Chapter Thirteen

The girls' bathroom near the Lincoln High cafeteria was packed. Girls jostled for the mirror. Brushes were borrowed. Lipsticks were compared. Makeovers were executed in five minutes' time.

By twelve-fifteen that Thursday afternoon, Daly was ready to kill whoever had invented hair spray, the curling iron, eyeliner, blush, and the whole concept of makeup.

"There she is." Sophy grabbed Daly's arm and pulled her around the corner, away from the sinks. Daly barely had time to glimpse Laverne before she ducked into one of the stalls that lined the far wall. She and Sophy had talked it over the night before. They'd decided that Laverne was wrong, and Sophy's grandmother was right. Laverne wasn't being heroic in shielding her friend. She was acting dumb, and hurting herself, the school, and the rest of her friends. Now their job was to convince her of that. She wouldn't listen to Peter, or her Dad, or the Ivanovs, but maybe she'd listen to her friends.

"What will we say?" Daly asked Sophy in a whisper.

"Whatever it takes to get her to face up to the fact she has to give in to Peter." Sophy sounded so definite. Still, Daly had to agree. Laverne had managed to avoid everyone from the Academy ever since Peter and her dad had grounded her. Mrs. B., their housekeeper, was actually driving her to school and picking her up. Still, Laverne herself must have been working very hard at not being seen around the corridors of the school. Daly had no classes with her, and neither did Sophy, but usually they passed each other between periods in the hall, changing classrooms.

Laverne came out of the stall and headed for the sink. Daly quietly marched up on one side of her, Sophy on the other. Laverne looked up from soaping her hands and started at the sight of their faces in the mirror.

"What do you want?" she said after a minute. A school bell rang, and the crowd in the restroom thinned.

Sophy handed her a towel. Daly folded her arms and told her, "We need to talk."

"I'm not talking. Orders from on high!" she said sarcastically. "I'm not to—let's see, how exactly did MacGregor put it?—*fraternize* with the other students while on probation." She glared at Daly, then at Sophy in turn. "I might contaminate you." She tried to push past Daly. "Would you mind?" she asked, waiting for Daly to move.

Daly stood her ground. "Look, Laverne. None of us think what you did was that bad—"

"I'm touched," Laverne replied with scorn. She

glared at each girl in turn, then shrugged. She plopped her embroidered backpack on the counter and pulled out a wide-toothed comb. She yanked it through her hair. Then jammed it back in her bag again. "Funny, I don't hear any talking going on."

"Stop it, Laverne. Don't make it harder for all of us," Sophy pleaded. "Look, I really respect that you don't want to get a friend in trouble, but now the whole school is up against the wall. I think you should just tell Peter or your father who was with you that night."

"What?" A look of real pain crossed Laverne's expressive face. "You're asking me to turn someone in? What kind of rat do you think I am?"

"You're no rat. The person who was with you is the real creep here," Daly exclaimed passionately. "She probably knows as well as we all do what's at stake."

"Does she?" Laverne scoffed. "Apparently, she doesn't care." She sounded so bitter and hurt, Daly wanted to just hug her. But Laverne had a real cold hands-off feel about her today.

"Maybe she does and is just scared," Sophy suggested gently. "Maybe you'd be doing her a favor. She probably feels so embarrassed and downright terrified by now that she can't even begin to imagine how she'd own up to being with you."

"Embarrassed? Scared?" Laverne actually laughed. "Not her. No way. She's probably relishing every minute of this."

"So if she's such a creep, why defend her?" Daly asked.

"Who's defending her? What she does or doesn't do is her business."

"Maybe," Sophy said, her voice hardening. "It's not just her business, or your business anymore, Laverne Grey. If this gala gets canceled, the school's future is up in the air again. Lots of rich people were supposed to come tomorrow night. We're supposed to be in the news, on TV. This is a really big deal—"

"You've sure changed your tune," Laverne said, regarding Sophy carefully. "Seems to me you weren't so hot on this project a few weeks ago."

"Well, I am now," Sophy stated.

"Besides, it's not just the school, Laverne. It's your future as a dancer," Daly pointed out.

Laverne shrugged lavishly. "What future? I'm no Sophy Bartlett," she said, meeting Sophy's eyes in the mirror. "Everyone thinks I'm a loser at the school. The only reason I'm there is because of my father—everyone thinks that."

"That's not true!" Daly cried. Sophy shook her head ruefully.

"Laverne, it's not just your future, it's ours, too."

"Too bad," Laverne snapped. She shouldered her bag. "You will just have to take care of the rest of 'us.' I'm going to look after number one from here on in." With that she shoved past Daly and out into the hall.

Daly looked helplessly at Sophy. "Now what? I have to call the papers and the cable station by four to let them know what's happening. Peter told me that the media committee had to take responsibility for notifying the press."

Sophy shook her head. "We tried our best. I'm not even sure you should wait until four."

"Might as well," Daly said with a defeated shrug. "Just in case Laverne's partner in crime has second thoughts at the last minute."

"Something about what Laverne said," Sophy mused as they left the bathroom and joined the stream of students heading for the classrooms. "I keep thinking I should know who her friend was."

"Some friend," Daly scoffed.

"Daly!" Sophy cried, suddenly looking inspired. "That's it. It's someone who's *not* a very good friend, and I have a pretty good idea what's going on here."

"You do? Who?" Daly felt the first faint stirs of hope.

"I'm not sure yet. But, listen," Sophy said, bolting toward the door, "don't call the cable station or Peter or anyone until you hear from me. I'll phone here before the afternoon's over."

♡ ♡ ♡

Twenty minutes later, Sophy jumped off the High Street bus. The stop was just across from Patel's curry place and the Rainbow School of Dance.

She hesitated before crossing the street. *What am*

I walking into? she wondered. She might be making a terrible mistake. On the other hand, it would be even worse not to risk it. A lot was on the line here. If she had guessed wrong, she'd have to live with a lot of nastiness—big-time nastiness. Still, it was worth it.

She hurried up the steps to the school. Compared to the last time she'd been inside, on open-studio night, the place was almost like a tomb. No one was at the front desk. Typing came from the office, and the sound of voices came from another room further down the empty hall. It was peaceful, appealing, a place with good vibes. From the studio at the end of the corridor, Sophy heard strains of dance music. After a moment she recognized the familiar tune. "As Time Goes By," the theme from *Casablanca*, her all-time favorite tearjerker.

She approached the studio quietly. Halfway up the studio walls were windowed glass. She hung back a little and peered inside. At least she had guessed right so far. Roxanna and Carlos hadn't been at school today. Inez had mentioned something about an upcoming competition. A really big one. Sophy had figured to find them here, on release time, working.

They were dancing to the 1940s song. Sophy had no idea what the dance itself was called, she only knew it was lovely, simply lovely. Roxanna was dressed in a worn-looking but still glamorous filmy yellow dress. It came down midway to her calves, and gossamer scarflike pieces went from the top of the bodice down to her wrists. The fabric floated and flowed with her every move.

The couple moved with great grace around the studio, and Sophy found herself transported from the dingy mirrored space to a glamorous ballroom. They were looking at each other with such intensity, such joy.

How could Carlos not fall in love with her? How could any guy not melt being next to her? This was beyond romantic, this was the stuff great love stories were made of. Between the music, the dress, the incredible beauty of the dance, Sophy was moved to tears. One stole down her cheek.

Then suddenly Roxanna stopped dead and stamped one high-heeled foot. "Really, Vargas, you are totally out of it," she charged. Her voice was harsh and grated like chalk on a blackboard.

The spell was broken. Sophy's tears dried right up. Without giving herself time to think, or change her mind, or lose her nerve, she marched into the room.

"Sophy?" Carlos took a step toward her. "What are you doing here?"

Sophy barely acknowledged his presence. Her business wasn't with him.

"Roxanna Ivanov," she said, trying to keep her voice steady. "You're the girl, aren't you? The one who was with Laverne the other night."

Roxanna's haughty expression fell. Only for a second, but it was enough.

"Admit it!" Sophy charged.

"Admit what?" Roxanna laughed. "You think *I'd* risk that kind of scandal to hang out at some dumb club? Come off it, Sophy. I think you know me better than that. I'm not self-defeating like Laverne."

Sophy wavered. The girl was ambitious, smart, and cunning. Too calculating about her future to risk breaking the law and getting caught at it. Sophy took a good, hard look at the Russian girl. She seemed so much older, so much more in-the-know than any of Sophy's friends.

But she, too, was only seventeen or so. Maybe she wasn't as together as she seemed.

"Tell her, Carlos. You've known me forever." Roxanna stomped over to the stand holding the sound system and flicked the music off. Only then did Sophy realize the old tune had been playing in the background.

Carlos shrugged. "It's not exactly Roxy's style," he started to say, then Sophy watched as a frown crossed his face. "But, Roxanna," he said as she crossed the studio heading back toward them. "Are you sure you don't know something about this?"

Roxanna stopped dead in her tracks. She planted her hands on her hips and looked really hurt. "I can't believe you. Why would I know a thing about that Laverne person?"

"Until this mess came up, 'that Laverne person' was starting to hang with you," Sophy pointed out. "I thought you two were friends."

"I don't make friends that quickly." Roxanna boasted.

I bet you don't, Sophy retorted silently, and wondered exactly what friends Roxanna did have. She seldom saw her socializing at school.

"I don't waste time with just anyone."

"Laverne isn't just anyone," Carlos said in a soft, angry voice. "I don't see how you can put her down like this, Roxanna. She hasn't done anything to you."

"That's true." Roxanna admitted readily. "But that doesn't mean I know what's going on in her head. Who her friends are." She smoothed a wrinkle in her silky skirt. "I don't hang out at salsa clubs, drinking."

"Neither does Laverne, usually," Sophy spoke up quickly. "She's unpredictable and a practical joker, and does get in trouble, but not like this. Not as long as I've known her. I just think it's a funny coincidence Roxanna, that the minute you get tight with her, she ends up at a club in this sort of trouble."

"I'm not the only new person Laverne has met lately. How about Inez? Or Aiko?"

Carlos bristled. "Leave Inez out of this. Besides, even with makeup you know she couldn't pass for twenty-one. Not like you." Carlos stopped talking and just stared at Roxanna. Sophy watched as a look of disbelief, then disappointment crossed his face. "It *was* you!" he cried, realization dawning on him. "Sophy's right. But it's like that time in Philadelphia—"

"Carlos, *don't*—!"

Carlos ignored Roxanna's frantic cry and plunged ahead as Sophy looked on, not quite sure what was happening. "You wanted to push the envelope to see if you could really pass for older."

"And it worked, didn't it? What did I have to prove here?"

"Who knows, but you dragged Laverne along."

So Sophy's hunch had been right. An immense sense of relief washed over her. She started to say something, but Carlos was still raging at Roxanna. "Then you left her at the club. You didn't care what happened to her—"

"That's not true. I didn't leave her, I helped—" Roxanna clapped her hand over her mouth.

The door to the studio opened. Nadia Ivanov stalked in. "What's the meaning of all this shouting?"

Peter was right behind her, putting on his jacket. He looked from Roxanna to Carlos to Sophy. "Sophy Bartlett, how come you're not in school?"

"I had to find out the truth," Sophy spoke up, feeling triumphant. "About Laverne. It was Roxanna. She was the other girl."

"What's this?" Nadia turned on Sophy. "You have the nerve to accuse my daughter of being some kind of criminal?"

"She's no criminal, Mrs. Ivanov," Carlos said stepping closer to Sophy. "Roxanna did no more, no less than Laverne. Except she didn't have the guts to speak up."

"Laverne? The girl who went to that club? You're trying to tell me Roxanna was there with her?" The woman began to smile.

Before anyone else could speak, Roxanna blurted, "Sophy is just trying to cover for"—she hesitated—"for herself, of course."

"What?!" Sophy, Peter, and Carlos cried in unison.

"Sophy?" Peter looked aghast, then put his hands on Sophy's shoulders and made her face him. "Is this true?"

Sophy stared helplessly at Peter. Peter MacGregor, her beloved teacher. Just the thought that he'd accuse her broke her heart.

Carlos stepped in. "No. It's not true. Sophy would never do something like that."

"And Roxanna would?" Nadia let out a tight laugh. "Please, Carlos, do not take me for a fool," she said.

"Roxanna would what?" Everyone turned. Mikhail Ivanov had walked into the room. He was carrying a thermos bottle and was wearing a University Heights Taxi baseball cap.

"Carlos and this Sophy girl are trying to tell me that it was our Roxanna who lied about her age, went to the club that night with the other girl, and was involved with that fight."

Sophy hadn't said all that, but if Mrs. Ivanov wanted to lay it all on Roxanna, Sophy was of a mind to let her. As far as she knew, neither girl was involved in any fight.

"Roxanna?" Mikhail repeated, then looked from Sophy to Carlos, but finally his gaze rested on his daughter. "So, that explains it," he said quietly.

"Explains what, exactly?" Roxanna said, tapping her foot. "Really, Father, you make such a mystery out of everything."

"Ah, but the mystery is solved," he said. "She's right," he declared, pointing at Sophy. "Roxanna must be the girl."

"How do you know, Mikhail?" Peter asked.

"Because Laverne mentioned when she got into the cab that night that her friend had not waited for a cab. She did not want to take one and how stupid that was when it was late and dark and she'd have to walk or take a bus back downtown. Until now," he said apologetically, "I had forgotten about that."

"This is sick," Nadia exclaimed. "You do not even defend your own daughter?"

Mikhail shrugged. "There is nothing to defend. She is as wrong as the other girl."

"But I don't understand," Peter said. "Why wouldn't Roxanna want to take a cab?"

"Because she was afraid I might pick her up. She knew I would recognize her."

"Daddy, stop." Roxanna's voice trembled, and she looked like she wanted to die.

Sophy looked at Mikhail, then understood. Of course. He was a cab driver. Roxanna probably would die before anyone knew that. Though why she should care was beyond Sophy. Her uncle Evan worked for a cab company that serviced the airport.

All at once Sophy felt sorry for her. Roxanna looked freaked and positively mortified.

"So, Roxanna, what do you have to say about this now?" asked Peter.

Roxanna's dusky cheeks paled slightly. She lowered her eyes and spoke through gritted teeth. "Okay, it was me. I went with Laverne, but"—she looked up, directly at Carlos, and two angry spots burned on her cheeks—"I didn't leave her there. I got Laverne out of that club, or she might have gotten hurt. She didn't start the fight. Neither did I. Laverne had just one beer and sort of lost it. But it wasn't our fault."

"I cannot believe I am hearing this." Nadia sat heavily on a chair. "I am not sure what to do about it, either."

Sophy fought her urge to hang around, to find out what would happen to Roxanna. She wanted to be sure that whatever happened, Roxy would have to suffer at least as much as Laverne. That was only fair. But right now, she had to get to a phone and call Daly.

"So, Peter," Sophy said, putting her hand on his arm, "the gala? Is it on?"

Peter nodded. "It's on."

Chapter Fourteen

Sophy swept out of the room right past Carlos. He looked after her, tempted to follow, but he couldn't bear to leave Roxanna to face the music by herself.

He was furious at her. How could she sink so low? How could she let Laverne take the heat alone? Friends didn't treat each other that way. Decent people didn't treat a dog that way.

As he watched, Roxanna's face crumpled, and she broke down. She sank down in front of one of the chairs, pillowed her head in her arms on the seat, and wept. Her father looked away. Her mother looked disgusted. As angry as he was, Carlos couldn't stand it. He walked up and put his hand on Roxanna's shoulder. She shrank from his touch.

"Go away," she sobbed, then looked up, tears streaking her makeup. "I hope you're happy now. You and your precious *Sophy!*" She fairly spat Sophy's name. Carlos felt as if she'd slapped him.

"So what do we do with her?" Nadia asked Peter. Carlos stiffened at Nadia's tone. The woman was a regular witch sometimes. She was talking about her daughter, who was in trouble and freaked out, as if she were some kind of object. The woman was so cold, Carlos's blood chilled just thinking about the punishment she might inflict on Roxy now.

Peter's response was instant. "Same as with Laverne. She can't come to classes. Can't perform in the gala."

"Not perform in the gala?" Carlos repeated, horrified. "No. That's not right."

"*Now* you stand up for me. After you tricked me back there with Sophy," Roxanna charged. "What kind of friend are you, anyway?"

Carlos wheeled around and exclaimed angrily, "The best friend you've got right now, so just keep quiet."

He turned back to Peter. "You really can't mean this. I know you want to be fair to Laverne and all, but she's not the performer Roxanna is. She's not as important to the program tomorrow night."

"That would not be fair to the other girl," Mikhail stated flatly.

"There you go again, Dad. It's like you could care less about what happens to me," Roxanna accused.

"But Carlos is right," Nadia said, nodding thoughtfully. "The school needs to show off its best students. Just like Sophy Bartlett is your best ballet student, Roxanna and Carlos are our best junior couple."

Carlos crossed his fingers. Maybe Peter would listen to Nadia.

He felt rather than saw Sophy come back into the

room. "What are you saying?" Sophy spoke up, her voice shaking slightly. "That Roxanna should be able to perform, while Laverne can't?"

"Sophy, this is none of your business," Peter said firmly.

"Yes, it is. When you guys decided to join the schools, it became everyone's business. Everyone who goes there, anyway. If Roxanna performs, then Laverne should, too. If Laverne is grounded and kept out of the show, ground Roxanna, keep her home. That's only fair."

"What's fair isn't the point here," Carlos spoke up. "It's what's best for the gala—for the new school. Whatever you decide to do with Roxanna, do it after the gala. But let me dance with her tomorrow night. Without her, the show will be weaker. We need to put our best foot forward. She's one of the best we've got."

Roxanna cast an adoring look at Carlos.

Peter and Mikhail exchanged a glance. Peter cleared his throat. "Sorry, Carlos. I see your point. I am half in agreement with you, but what these two girls did was serious. Now they have to suffer the consequences. If they had given half a thought to the good of the school before they had gone out on their little escapade, none of us would be here having this discussion."

Carlos stood a little taller. "You mean I won't get to dance with Roxanna tomorrow night?"

"No, you won't," Peter reiterated.

Carlos shook his head and moved to leave the room. As he passed Sophy, he caught the expression on her face. "You don't have to gloat. It's everyone's loss. We really needed her at the gala," he said, loud enough for only her to hear.

"Believe me," Sophy countered coolly, "we'll manage quite well without her, thank you."

♡ ♡ ♡

"Being grounded is going around like some kind of virus," Sophy complained to Daly on the phone late that night. Her mother was still out. It was the last night of the weeklong seminar sponsored by the literature department. A cocktail party followed by a banquet at Le Coq D'Or would keep her mother out past midnight.

"Who's grounded now? Besides Roxanna and Laverne?" Daly inquired.

"Yours truly," Sophy grumbled, trying not to strangle herself with the phone cord as she squirmed, one arm at a time, into her nightshirt.

On the other end of the phone Daly gasped. "What did *you* do?"

Sophy actually wished she *had* done something ground-worthy. She pulled the scrunchy out of her ponytail and combed her fingers through her hair. "It's more like what I didn't do. Mr. Cunningham told Mom at parents' night that I still hadn't handed my Jane Austen paper in."

Daly made a sympathetic sound. "I should be

grateful for small blessings. At least my mother isn't a lit professor."

"So outside of the gala, I'm kind of stuck here for two weeks." Sophy flopped down with her head hanging over the edge of the bed, the ends of her hair just brushing the floor.

"Two weeks? That's really stiff, and—" Daly's voice was interrupted by a double beep. "Daly, hold on a sec. Call Waiting. Mom is probably checking up to be sure I haven't headed off, inspired by Laverne, to Tangos and Sauce."

"Don't even kid about that!" Daly exclaimed.

"Hang on," Sophy said, cutting her off. She pressed the receiver button. "Mom?"

"Sophy?" a deep male voice asked.

Sophy grit her teeth. "Carlos? How'd you get my number?" she asked.

"I—we exchanged them at the first rehearsal, I think." He sounded unsure of himself and defensive all at once. The boy was maddening. Positively maddening.

"It's late. What do you want?" she asked, then remembered Daly on the other line. Well, she'd get rid of Carlos fast, and—

"Not far from here, and—"

What? What was he talking about? Sophy sat up on the bed. "Carlos, I didn't catch that."

"I said, I'm parked a block or so away. I need to see you."

"Now?" Sophy gasped. "But it's late, and—"

"Please," he said. "I need to talk in person, and—Sophy, I hate the phone. Besides, my quarter's going to run out."

Right, he was on a pay phone. "Hold on," she said, then pressed the receiver button again.

"You won't believe who that is on the other line," she blurted to Daly.

"Who?"

"Carlos Vargas. He wants to see me."

"Now?!" Daly sounded stunned.

"If Mom found out, I'd be grounded for the next year, or worse—"

"That's pretty bad," said Daly. After a moment she added, "Sophy, I think you should see him. Your mom will be out until one or so. Chance it. What's to lose? Maybe he wants to talk to you about Roxanna, what happened today at Rainbow Dance. Besides, you guys have to learn to iron out your differences and work together. Tomorrow you even have to dance together for the fund-raiser. Or have you forgotten?"

"How could I? I just wish it were the day after tomorrow and it were all over," Sophy said tightly. Then she remembered Carlos's quarter. "Look, he's on a pay phone." Frantically she asked Daly, "What should I do?"

"See him."

Sophy nodded. Then she said good-bye to Daly and pressed the receiver button again. "Carlos?" She half hoped he had hung up.

"Sophy? Can I come over?"

"Yeah. For a few minutes, but you'd better just come to the backyard. Meet me by the swing set. I'll be down in a sec."

A few minutes later she was downstairs at the kitchen door, zipped up in her long velour robe. She waited at the half-open door until she saw Carlos's truck pull up. He parked a little down the block. She started out the door, then looked at her feet. She was wearing her bunny rabbit slippers. *He'll think I'm a regular dork!* she thought, and kicked them off. Barefoot, she tiptoed onto the back porch and down the short flight of creaky wooden steps.

She stepped into the damp grass and thanked the goddess of weather that so far, autumn hadn't been cold.

"Sophy?" Carlos called from over by the rose-bushes.

"Yeah," she said. She stepped up to the swing set, self-conscious about her clothes.

He came out of the shadows. His shoulders straight, his back proud, he looked right at her, cool as water. As if he were used to talking to girls in bathrobes by moonlight.

"So?" she asked, folding her arms tightly across her chest.

He shrugged. For a second he didn't look so confident. "I didn't like what happened today," he said finally, sitting down on one of the swings. "You seemed freaked that I thought Roxanna should still be part of the fund-raiser. And I wanted to explain what was going on there—"

Sophy moistened her lips. "I'm listening," she said.

"Roxanna's just my partner, Sophy. She's just a . . . a friend," he seemed to be experimenting with the word. "That's all. Whatever you or Daly or the other girls think of her—and believe me, she really loused up with Laverne—that doesn't change the fact she's an incredible dancer. We work well together."

Sophy knew he was right. "But that's not the point," she said, surprised by how strong she sounded. How sure she felt. "If Laverne can't be in the fund-raiser, Roxanna shouldn't be, either. Laverne had a lot to contribute, too. Sure, she's not as flashy a dancer as Roxanna, but when it comes to ballet, she's talented. Besides, she put the whole thing together"—Sophy bit her lip. She heaved a loud sigh. "Why am I defending her?" She chafed her arms and looked off into the shadows and wondered when her life had suddenly stopped being so simple.

"Because you're her friend." Carlos made it sound so reasonable. "She made a mistake, she's being punished for it. Anyway, neither of them are going to be in the show, no matter what either of us thinks. I just came to say we've got to dance together tomorrow night, and I wanted to clear the air. I'm tired of fighting with you, Sophy."

Something in his voice made her look at him. He patted the swing next to his. "Bet I can swing higher than you."

Sophy hesitated, then returned his smile. "Bet you can't!"

She jumped on the swing and began pumping hard with her legs. Her long robe tangled in her legs. She stopped, hitched it up above her knees, and tried again. In a few strong pumps of her muscular legs she was almost as high as Carlos.

They looked across at each other and suddenly started laughing. "Ever try this?" Carlos asked and, before she could answer, he stood up. The swing was going so high, so fast, Carlos's head was brushing the leaves on the lower branches of the tree.

"Carlos, be careful," she cried, then remembered to lower her voice. "Don't get hurt. I need my partner for tomorrow night."

He shrugged and, timing the arc of the swing perfectly, hopped off and scurried out of the way as it careened emptily toward him.

Sophy slowed down, but he stepped behind her and began pushing her swing. She leaned back and stopped pumping, enjoying the sensation of having him push her higher and higher. "It's been ages since I've done this," he said, a light, happy note in his voice.

"Not as long as it's been since I've been 'swung.'" She laughed. "I'm the older sister. When we still used this set, I was always pushing my kid sister."

"How many do you have—brothers and sisters?" Carlos asked.

Sophy couldn't believe he didn't know. Then she realized she didn't know much about him, either, in spite of all of their working together. She told him about Emma.

She already knew Inez, but learned about his two older brothers: Oswaldo and Luis. "They're the good eggs. I'm the rotten one of the bunch," he said, giving the swing a harder push. She could feel his anger.

"Because you dance?"

"Because I *live* to dance. Everyone wants me to be something else. Mom wants college; Dad for me to go to some kind of tech or trade school so I can help with his business. Sometimes I just want to pick up and leave and head somewhere else."

Sophy thought back to her own threats to leave home "I've felt that way, too," she said softly. "My mom's into this college thing. But if I want to be a ballerina, I can't stop for school now. I have to start auditioning—"

"That must go over like a ton of bricks. And your dad, what does he say?"

Sophy's mouth went dry. Her dad. Was she ready to talk about him with a stranger? With Carlos Vargas? "Not much," was all she could come up with. But her voice caught a bit.

The swing slowed. It spun a little to the right,

then to the left. Sophy dragged her foot on the ground to make it stop. The grass was dewy and cold on her bare toes, but she hardly noticed. Carlos came around the front of the swing and steadied the chains with his hands.

He was looking at her, puzzled. "We're not as different as I thought," he said, sounding a little surprised.

"No, we aren't," she admitted. "And I'm sorry that it took a while to figure that out, Carlos." It was time for a clean slate. It was time to start over.

Carlos didn't say anything more. A breeze blew up, stirring the trees above their heads. In the moonlight the shadow of branches played on his face. A few leaves drifted down around them. He reached out and brushed one out of her hair. At his touch, Sophy's insides melted right down. She yearned to reach up, to take his head in her hands and draw him close enough to kiss.

Except she'd never kissed a guy or been kissed. She hated that fact. Sweet sixteen, and she felt like a walking fool.

She didn't know what to do, if kissing him first were right or wrong. She tried to picture screen kisses. When Juliet kissed Romeo, who did what first? But she couldn't remember one love scene. And then Carlos was so close, she could smell the dark scent of his shampoo, the clean, soapy smell of his skin. She caught her breath just as his lips brushed hers, and she suddenly almost couldn't remember her own name.

His kiss was light and feathery. Her hands hung limp at her side, unable to move; her heart slowed, everything slowed, she was barely breathing. Then he leaned back ever so slightly, and the look in his eyes was so direct, so searching. She felt as if she suddenly had no secrets left. Part of her wanted to run away, back to the house, to the safety of her room.

But her feet seemed to have grown roots right where she was. When he kissed her again, it was different. His mouth met hers, and his kiss was strong. Without thinking, she put her hands on the sides of his face and kissed him back, heart and soul. The ground seemed to spin beneath her; the breath whooshed right out of her. Then, as fast as it all started, it stopped. Carlos stepped back, at arm's length.

The color rushed to Sophy's face. *Did I do it wrong?* she wondered frantically, touching her lips and glad for the dark. She felt so inexperienced, so incredibly embarrassed.

"Sophy," he said, a catch in his voice. At first he kept looking at her, his dark eyes unreadable. But finally he lowered his gaze and stared at his feet. He kicked the soft earth with the pointy toe of his boot. "Sorry," he said hoarsely, taking another step back. One more step and he'd fall into the rosebush. "I shouldn't have done that."

Sophy opened her mouth to tell him, *Yes. Yes, you should have.* If this is what kissing felt like, she adored it. He didn't give her a chance to say a word.

"We're partners. And—um—partners shouldn't get involved." He paced a few steps down the lawn, then came right back.

Have you told Roxanna that? Sophy wondered, but kept her mouth shut. It didn't take a brain surgeon to figure out Roxanna thought of herself as *very* involved with Carlos Vargas.

Meanwhile, Carlos was talking as if he'd memorized his speech from a book on ballroom etiquette. "In ballroom dancing, generally, people try not to be involved with their partners—I mean, sometimes they are. But if the romance breaks up, everything goes down the tubes. It's too tough working together with all that bad history."

Why did the history have to be bad? Sophy wondered, her hand drifting again to her lips. They were still tingling. Her heart was pounding so hard, she couldn't believe Carlos couldn't hear it. What in the world was he talking about? She couldn't believe he wasn't feeling the same way she did. As if every pore of her body was alive, electric, charged with energy.

"Carlos?" she managed finally. "I don't get it. We're not real partners. We're—"

"Friends," he said firmly. "Please, Sophy, let's be friends."

Friends. The way he said it was like the period

at the end of a sentence. Sophy swallowed hard. All at once she realized she was standing in the backyard, barefoot, with a bathrobe over her nightshirt, alone with a guy. *Kissing a guy!* What had she been thinking of? She suddenly clutched the collar of her robe tighter around her.

"Someone's coming," Carlos exclaimed, ducking back into the shadows.

Sophy heard the crunch of gravel in the driveway before she saw the reflection of headlights in the kitchen windows just above them. "Mom's home," she cried. "I'd better get in." She started for the door, then paused with one foot on the bottom step of the short flight leading up to the back porch. "Friends," she stated, trying the idea out.

"Friends." He sounded sad, but then he repeated firmly, "Yes. Friends. Can we do that?"

Sophy nodded, afraid to trust her voice.

Out front the car door slammed. Sophy turned quickly and tiptoed up the steps. Quietly she cracked open the kitchen door and slipped through. She hurried to the fridge and flung it open just as her mother switched on the kitchen light.

"Sophy?" Her mother sounded startled. "What are you doing in here? Barefoot? In the dark?"

Sophy looked down at her feet; a blade of grass was plastered on her right big toe. She tucked her foot up under her robe and mumbled, not able yet to face her mother. "Starving. I'm absolutely starving."

"You're so lucky," her mother sighed, tossing

down her briefcase and purse and hanging her trench coat on the rack by the door. "You can eat a house and not gain weight! But you'd better get to bed. It's really late."

"Right, Mom." Sophy pressed her head against the freezer to cool down her hot cheeks. Finally, she faced her mother.

Her mother stared at her hard from the kitchen door. Suddenly she wondered if being kissed showed. "Why, Sophy, you look so pretty tonight."

A blush coursed from Sophy's neck right up to her forehead. "Uh—thanks!" she managed, then raced past her mother up to her room. She closed the door behind her and pressed her back against it. She felt her face. Her cheeks were almost too hot to touch. Suddenly her chest tightened, and she didn't know if she were going to laugh or cry.

The sound of footsteps drew her to the window. She looked out. A lone figure was heading down the sidewalk, away from her house. It was Carlos. He stopped beneath the streetlight and fiddled with his keys. Then he crossed the deserted street to his truck.

He opened the door but, before getting in, he looked back at her house. He didn't glance up to the second floor. He didn't know where her room was. He leaned up against the open door and watched her house a long time. Then his shoulders lifted in a visible sigh, and he climbed in and turned on the ignition. The taillights went on and stained the pavement red. Pulling away, he stopped at the light, then made a right at the corner. She could hear the engine drone as he downshifted on the steep hill. Sophy pressed her ear against the screen, listening until she couldn't hear him anymore.

Friends.

Maybe, she thought, that wasn't such a bad thing. One kiss had sent her soul reeling. One kiss had set off a whole explosion of feelings.

Feelings Sophy didn't know she had. Feelings she couldn't begin to understand.

Maybe being friends with Carlos was a safer way of beginning.

Chapter Fifteen

The next morning P. J. called an early rehearsal. "We've got a problem," he told everyone gathered on the stage of the Academy Theater. Vague grunts and yawns and only a couple of smart comments greeted his announcement. Inez was nodding off. Daly, who hated coffee, was already on her third cup. Sophy could barely keep her eyes open. Which was, she thought, absolutely perfect. With eyes closed she didn't have to even catch the smallest glimpse of Carlos.

After last night she had no idea how she'd face him today, let alone dance with him.

P. J. went on, anyway. "Everyone's heard about Roxanna Ivanov."

Hisses and boos met his remark.

"Quiet," P. J. said. "She and Laverne have enough to deal with. By the time they're back in class regularly, we'll be onto a brand-new scandal of the week," he joked. "But our problem is that without both of them, we're missing not one, but two dancers. Roxanna was in almost every number. There's no one to really fill in for her since, except for one piece early on, almost every other ballroom dancer is slated to share the stage with her. Time is short, so I decided the best way to solve it all is to cut down the length of the performance and rearrange numbers. Instead of closing with a mixed ballroom-ballet set, I decided we should close with the ballroom demonstration."

"What?" several voices objected. But Sophy spoke up. "Come on, everyone. This is an emergency. Besides, it doesn't matter so much what we close with as long as it's good."

P. J. flashed Sophy a big smile. "Glad you're game, Sophy, because you are a big part of this plan. That is"—he turned and searched the group gathered around him—"if Carlos cooperates."

Carlos? Sophy's eyes popped open. She regarded P. J. suspiciously.

"Game for what?" Carlos's voice came from somewhere in the shadow of the wings.

"Partnering Sophy in the ballroom finale!"

"WHAT!" they both shouted in unison.

"I can't perform a ballroom number in public," Sophy protested. "Besides, it isn't just one dance. You have a waltz, a tango, a rhumba, and a fox-trot. I don't even know what a fox-trot is."

"She's never even done half the dances," Carlos cried, stepping out of the wings. His hair looked mussed, he hadn't shaved yet, and Sophy found herself thinking that he looked perfectly adorable. As soon as the thought crossed her mind, she began to blush.

"Oh, but she can!" Inez spoke up. She sounded so enthusiastic, Sophy felt a little sick.

"All you have to do," Inez told Carlos, "is change the level of the dance. We'll do simpler versions. I don't mind, do you?" She looked around at her partner, Nick, at Aiko and Tommy. They all shook their heads.

"We could do fewer dances, too. . . ." Carlos mused aloud. "How about just waltz and tango? She already knows tango, and has probably waltzed some in ballet."

"Sophy?" Inez turned to her, a huge smile on her small face.

Sophy didn't know what to say. Like metal drawn to a magnet, she turned to Carlos.

He was standing a few feet off, hands in his pockets, looking sheepish and eager. "I'm all for it," he said, finally meeting her eyes. "We'll make it easy. But it will be beautiful, too."

Sophy felt as if he'd handed her a gift. "If Carlos thinks it can work, I'm all for it, too." She turned back to P. J. "If it'll help with the gala, hey, what's to lose?" she said, sounding more confident than she felt.

"I'll help you, too," Inez volunteered. "Me too!" said Aiko. "And we're the same size, so you can borrow one of my costumes. I'll go to Rainbow Dance later and pick one up."

"But we'd better get started," Inez said, jumping up and dusting off her jeans. "We've got about eight hours to get this scene together."

♡ ♡ ♡

Later on, looking back, Sophy couldn't believe that night. It was magical. It was scary. It was awful. It was perfect. It was sad Laverne never got to see it. It was too bad Roxanna did.

Sophy's *Sleeping Beauty* pas de deux with P. J. was the perfect show opener.

Inez's high-heeled vamp version of *Giselle* brought the house down.

Sophy and Carlos's *Tutus and Tangos* had the audience rolling in the aisles.

And Ray and Daly got a standing ovation for their *Bluebird Variation.*

Before Sophy knew it, time for the ballroom finale had come. Aiko had zipped up her dress. Aiko's older sister had basted the hem of the deep green tulle and organza sequined creation. But Sophy stood, knees shaking in the wings, wondering if she would turn her ankles waltzing in her heels.

To think only this morning she had been nervous about seeing Carlos, about dancing one dance with him tonight. But today it was as if last night hadn't happened. It was as if Carlos couldn't even remember they had kissed.

Which turned out for the best. There was no time for remembering. Not while they practiced all that waltzing.

"Remember," Carlos said, continuing to bombard her with instructions. Wearing a tuxedo, he looked formal, like a stranger. "Keep your chin up, maintain the frame and, above all, don't try to dance on your own. Just follow, Sophy. Follow."

"Carlos," she pleaded as she heard the audience from the other side of the curtain file back into their seats, "I can't do this."

"You have no choice. Just go out there. Feel as beautiful as you are. You'll do great."

"Places!" P. J. whispered loudly.

Carlos took her hand and brought her onstage. He helped her fluff out her dress. Then he assumed his best posture.

The curtain whooshed up. Sophy's knees began to give. Then the music started. Carlos waited a moment; then, his hand was firmly pressed against Sophy's back, and she found herself moving with him around the stage. At first her feet felt like lead, but as the waltz continued she found herself carried by the music, and by Carlos.

The music stopped, they held their final pose, then everything shifted to the tango. The music and the steps were more familiar to Sophy, and halfway through the number she found following Carlos had begun to feel more natural. She began to trust him as he guided her through the dance. Suddenly they were moving as one, to the music, with each other.

The music swelled then died then grew again. Finally, all too soon, the dance came to an end.

They held their pose, a theatrical dramatic tango hold. The audience roared with applause. The curtain fell. For a long second Sophy just held on to

Carlos. Then his hands tightened around her, and he brushed his lips on the top of her head. "Beautiful, Sophy." But she didn't know if he meant her or her dancing.

Abruptly the spell broke. Inez was hugging her; she was hugging Aiko. Tommy was hugging everyone, and then Ray and Daly bounded onto the stage. "You did it, Sophy. Roxanna's going to writhe with jealousy when she hears about it."

"*Hears* about it!" Will scorned. "I saw her out there. Front row center watching, with her mother. I guess the Ivanovs have a different definition of grounded."

Then Peter appeared and gathered them together for curtain calls. The next day, Daly counted five of them. P. J. swore there were more. After two, Sophy had stopped counting.

After the last one, Peter called for silence. The curtain went up, and he stepped forward and grabbed a microphone, calling for everyone's attention.

"Tonight," he announced, his cheeks pink with excitement, his voice proud, "was a success. In more ways than one. These young dancers met obstacles in putting together this evening's gala event, obstacles that would have daunted the most sophisticated and well-staffed of professional companies. And I'm proud of them."

He paused as the audience cheered and applauded.

Sophy gripped Ray's hand on one side; Inez's on

the other. She felt happy to be part of this new thing, this school that had just been born. She had been part of giving it life.

Then Peter raised his hands for silence. "But for the schools to be truly joined, we need one last step."

"The name!" The dancers onstage nudged and whispered and jostled and giggled.

"We need to be called something. We invited all the students of the school and anyone else in the community under the age of eighteen to come up with suggestions. There were plenty of good ones. Lots of creative ones. And some that at least will keep us laughing. But the winner is"—and Peter made a big business of pulling an envelope out of his pocket—*"Dance Tech!"* The theater clapped enthusiastically.

"Dance Tech?" Sophy repeated and loved it.

"Not bad," Carlos said.

"Whose is it?" Daly asked, just as the general applause died down.

Peter answered her question. "We owe the new name to one of our own students: Inez Vargas!"

"INEZ!" the kids on the stage gasped, then began to clap.

Then everyone mobbed Inez, and in the crush Sophy lost Carlos. She found herself passed around like a package, for hugs, and good wishes. Meanwhile Peter invited the whole audience to retire to the atrium of the school and to stay for a dance party, catered gratis by Le Coq D'Or.

Families pressed backstage. Emma ran up to hug her. Her grandparents were there; her mother. She hugged them all, and they told her how much they adored her dancing. And even though Emma thought the waltz was corny, she pronounced Carlos was *very* cute.

Sophy finally ushered them away, down off the stage. She promised to meet them later when she had changed and was dressed for the party.

Someone in the hallway backstage helped her unzip the ballroom costume. But by the time she got to the women's changing room, it was empty. Sophy took off her makeup and scrubbed her face. But she kept on her stockings and heels and slithered into the slim blue sleeveless sheath her mother had bought her for the party. It was trendy, and new, and made her feel grown up. *That club would even let me in tonight,* she told her reflection in the mirror. She put her hand to her mouth and stifled a nervous giggle. She shouldn't even be thinking something awful like that.

She moistened her mouth, touched up her lip gloss, then hurried outside, wondering if Carlos would notice her new dress.

Already the rows of seats had been rolled out of the theater, and the huge side doors opened to the school's atrium. The space was huge, but already crowded.

Along the edge of the stage, long buffet tables

had been laid out. Le Coq D'Or had catered the food free. Arnie's Liquor Store had supplied wine, while FoodKing had supplied sodas. The spread was lavish, sumptuous, and a feast for the eye. But Sophy wasn't hungry. She searched the crowd for her mother, for Emma, for her grandparents, for Carlos.

The first person she saw was Roxanna.

"Hope you're satisfied," the girl said, walking up. "And close your mouth. Yes, it's me. I'm here. My mother pulled some strings. But don't worry about Laverne. I sort of spotted her, too. Maybe she's hiding out behind the seats. Or backstage somewhere. She does not have permission to be here. My mother made that perfectly clear."

"Whatever, Roxanna." Sophy just wanted to put as much distance as possible between them.

"Carlos is a dream to dance with," Roxanna said, tapping Sophy's wrist with a newly polished nail. "Your big moment with him has come and gone. Hope you enjoyed it while it lasted. Because believe me, you won't dance with him again." She melted back into the crowd before Sophy could even begin to think of some kind of reply.

Forget it, Sophy told herself. Why let the creep ruin her evening?

Someone had put on dance music. Surely Carlos would be there, on the dance floor. Couples were dancing to something mellow and slow. Emma was clomping back and forth from one side of the room to another with a girl her age, in time to the music.

Sophy wandered the crowd, looking for Carlos. He wasn't on the dance floor. Suddenly the light and fizzy feeling inside of Sophy evaporated. What could keep him from dancing? Had Roxanna cornered him?

She looked around again and saw Inez approaching.

"Sophy, this is my mother."

Inez had her arm through her mother's, a thin woman with Carlos's eyes and sculpted face. But she was tiny like Inez. "Glad to meet you," the small woman said politely. But something about her made Sophy feel cold. *She doesn't like me,* Sophy realized. She doesn't like what she sees when I dance with Carlos.

"Is your dad here as well?" Sophy asked, to make conversation. Inez warned her with a quick shake of her head. "Yes. He is talking to Carlos," Mrs. Vargas said with a slight accent. Then Peter MacGregor came up. He drew Mrs. Vargas away, asking Inez if he could speak with her mother alone.

Inez scooted off with Sophy. "What's happening with your dad and Carlos?" Sophy asked.

"Let's just say he wasn't thrilled to see him partnering you on pointe." Inez's eyes were bright with excitement, and her cheeks were pink. In her soft rose dress, she looked really pretty. Sophy wondered how she ever could have thought this girl was plain and mousy.

"Don't tell Carlos I told you, but things at home are getting worse."

"I know, he spoke with me—last night," Sophy said, again wondering exactly how much Carlos ever said to Inez.

"Yes, he told me, " Inez said. "He needed to apologize about Roxanna and the whole mess. After tonight I wish you could always be his partner," she said earnestly.

"But I'm a ballet dancer!" Sophy reminded her.

"I know. And Roxanna and he do work well together."

Then Sophy remembered about the contest. She congratulated her and said, "Where'd you ever come up with such a cool name for the school? *Dance Tech*. I love it!"

"Carlos," Inez said simply, her eyes dancing. "Dad's always on his case about technical school. I put dance and technical together and there you go— Dance Tech." Inez frowned. "The problem is, I don't need the prize." Just then Emma galumphed their way. "Now that's someone who could use some dance lessons!" Inez remarked.

Sophy cracked up. "That's my kid sister. And she hates dancing."

Inez twinkled. "Then I think I'm going to give my free lessons to her. Three months of ballroom lessons!" Inez put her hand on Sophy's arm. "Anyways, if you're looking for Carlos, he went off that way, with my dad. Interrupting those two might not be a bad thing," she said, a trace of worry in her voice.

Sophy wended her way across the room, stopping to say hello to Mr. and Mrs. Flanagan, then to shake Peter's hand. She finally made it through the crowd, out toward the west side of the atrium.

The door to the loading dock was open, and a cool, damp breeze from the river blew in.

She started out, but the sound of voices, raised in argument, stopped her.

One of them she recognized instantly. *Carlos!* He was arguing with another man. Sophy began to back away. *I shouldn't be here. I shouldn't hear this. It's too private.*

"*¡Olvídate del baile!*" the man said in a loud voice.

"Forget about dancing?" Carlos fumed. "Not on your life, Dad." The pain in Carlos's voice went right to Sophy's heart.

His father let out a barrage of Spanish words. His tone was bitter. Sophy had no idea what he was saying, but from Carlos's response she could tell this was a pretty heavy argument.

"What I do with my life is my choice—not yours. I have to live it how I want. Or why live at all?" Carlos cried.

"Sometimes I cannot believe you are my son! Luis, now *that* is a good son. You should learn from your brother. He never would talk to me this way. *Never.*"

Carlos had told her about Luis last night. He

was the one who owned the hamburger joint.

"I am not like Luis. I can't live his life."

"I do not want you to live his life," his father declared passionately. "I want you only to leave this dream alone. To look at the world. It is a hard place. It is not a place for parties and dancing and all these prizes you wish you win! And do not tell me now about Olympics. That is a another dream. What you need is a trade. Next year I want you to come work with me in the shop. I tell you this a hundred times. You think you know better than your dad, but you know nothing."

"I only know that the shop was *your* dream, Papa, not mine. You have your dreams. My dreams are different."

"Dreams? Dreams don't feed a family. Dreams don't make a man of you. *Tu sueño es solo una ilusión.*"

"Wrong, Dad," Carlos shouted. "Just drop it! Nothing you say or do is going to change my mind."

"We'll see about that!" his father fumed. Then a wiry man pushed past Sophy, glaring at the floor. He passed without seeing her. But she watched him march into the room and head straight for Mrs. Vargas.

Sophy hesitated at the open door, not sure if Carlos wanted to be alone or with someone. She fingered the fabric of her dress and took a deep breath. "Carlos?" she called out into the night. But the music was loud, and he couldn't possibly hear her. Her arms were bare, and the breeze from the river was cool. For the first time there was a touch of fall in the air.

Sophy made up her mind. She stepped out onto the loading dock. The concrete platform was dark, lit only from lights in the parking lot. At first she didn't see anyone. Had Carlos left?

Her eyes adjusted to the half-light. A figure was sitting on the top step of the short flight of metal stairs leading down to the tarmac. His shoulders were hunched. For a minute she couldn't believe it was Carlos. He always stood and sat so tall, so proud.

"Carlos," she repeated, a little louder, afraid to intrude. She felt awkward. Last night he had wanted to tell her everything. But that was before they had kissed. Before he had pulled back and told her the kisses didn't count. They were outside the fence of friendship.

Now last night felt like a dream. Was she intruding? Did what happen last night give her the right to see him upset like this? Sophy suddenly had no choice. He looked awful, even from behind. She couldn't bear just to leave him like this. "Carlos!" This time her voice was loud and clear.

At the sound of his name, he straightened right up. "Sophy," he said, turning toward her. His expression flowed from pain to sorrow to a look that took her breath away. "Where were you?"

"I couldn't find you," she said. "The curtain fell, and there was so much commotion."

"True." He paused. "Out here, too. That was my dad. Or didn't you hear?"

"It was hard not to," she said. "He'll come round, Carlos. The Ivanovs will convince him. Peter will convince him."

"Maybe. Maybe," He said. He sounded a little tired. Then he shrugged and smiled right at Sophy. "But, hey, we did it. The gala was a hit. We've got a new school. Dance Tech!" he said the name, trying it out.

"Yeah," Sophy said. "Who would have thought Inez would come up with that one?"

"Can't figure where she got it from," Carlos said. So Inez hadn't told him about their dad being a kind of weird inspiration for the school's name. "What's she going to do with those free dance lessons?"

"Try charity—as in giving them to my kid sister, who hates dancing more than liver and onions!"

Carlos threw back his head and laughed. Suddenly Sophy saw the moon was still bright, the stars were out, and it was a beautiful night after all.

"I'd like to meet your sister," he said. "Maybe I'll ask her to dance."

"Now that might change her mind about partners. According to her, you're the local hunk of the middle-school set. Some sixth graders prefer you to Brad Pitt!"

"Only some?" Carlos sounded offended.

"Sorry, Carlos, only some."

"Guess I'm losing it!"

They both laughed lightly, then fell silent. Sophy stood, uncertain what to do. Carlos didn't make a move toward her. He seemed content sitting on the step.

She waited a moment, then crossed the loading dock. Carefully smoothing her dress, she sat down beside him. The cold metal chilled her legs, and she shivered.

Carlos casually rested his arm around her shoulder. "It's cold out here. We should get back in." He didn't draw her closer. He didn't hug her. But his hand was warm as toast against her bare skin.

"Your family all here, I mean besides Emma?"

Sophy hesitated. "Yes, everyone. My grandparents, my mother." She stopped.

He looked at her. He picked it up quickly. She hadn't mentioned her father. "Divorced?"

"Divorced," she answered. She liked that, a person who didn't ask for more than she was ready to give.

"So do I get to meet them?" he asked after a long pause.

"Sure. I mean, they'd love that. They all wondered who my partner was."

"Come on," he said, standing suddenly and taking her hand.

She held her breath, wondering what was next, as he pulled her to her feet.

But he began snapping the fingers of his other hand to the beat of a salsa tune wafting out the door.

either moving across the floor, or in place. When performed on pointe by a ballerina, they often give the impression of gliding smoothly across the floor.

Corps de ballet. Members of the ballet company who are not soloists.

Demi plié. Ballet exercise, usually done at the barre, performed by bending the knees as far as possible to either side while leaving the heels on the floor.

Milonga. An Argentinean dance from the late 1800's that predates the tango; the historic predecessor of the tango. The milonga can also be the dance salon where people dance tango.

Ochos. Translated from the Spanish, means "eight." One of the basic steps in Argentinean tango, where the feet trace a figure eight on the floor.

Pas de deux. A dance for two dancers. ("Pas de trois" means a dance for three dancers, and so on.)

Pointe. Exercises performed in pointe (or toe) shoes.

Rond de jambe a terre. A barre exercise performed to loosen the hip joint: performed first outward (en dehors) and then inward (en dedans).

Rosin. A sticky resin that ballet dancers use on the bottom of their shoes to help them grip the floor. Rosin is usually kept in a box in the ballet studio, or in the wings off stage. Ballerinas are sure to coat the tips of their toe-shoes with rosin to gain friction during their turns on pointe.

Salsa. (also known as the Mambo) A type of Latin dance music with complex rhythms and the dance that is done to that music.

Swing. Type of Jazz music, often played by Big Bands, that was originally popular in the 1930-40s and the dance that accompanied it. Types of swing include the Lindy, Jitterbug, Savoy, Smooth, and West Coast styles.

Tango. A romantic couples dance from Argentina characterized by dramatic, poetic movement and passion. Also refers to the music for the dance.